The Masters of Hope

The Masters of Hope

Carmel Kennedy

AuthorHouse™
1663 Liberty Drive
Bloomington, IN 47403
www.authorhouse.com
Phone: 1-800-839-8640

© 2011 by Carmel Kennedy. All rights reserved.

No part of this book may be reproduced, stored in a retrieval system, or transmitted by any means without the written permission of the author.

First published by AuthorHouse   11/09/2011

ISBN: 978-1-4670-7097-3 (sc)
ISBN: 978-1-4670-7096-6 (hc)
ISBN: 978-1-4670-7095-9 (ebk)

Library of Congress Control Number: 2011919097

Printed in the United States of America

Any people depicted in stock imagery provided by Thinkstock are models, and such images are being used for illustrative purposes only.
Certain stock imagery © Thinkstock.

This book is printed on acid-free paper.

Because of the dynamic nature of the Internet, any web addresses or links contained in this book may have changed since publication and may no longer be valid. The views expressed in this work are solely those of the author and do not necessarily reflect the views of the publisher, and the publisher hereby disclaims any responsibility for them.

Prologue

Year 2320

The world has changed. No one knew exactly how or why but there is a cloud, no, more like a type of haze over everything: everyone. The family nucleus has been extended or totally eliminated, depending on how you look at it. The schools are where a child exists, and Mom and Dad are only memories, at best, that some experience in dreams.

But once it is found that these memories may be coming forward the offenders disappear. No one knows where the offenders go or what becomes of them. With no parents to demand answers it is simply forgotten and life goes on.

Until 'she' comes along. Her description is vague. The 'masters' are not aware of her yet but they can feel that a change is evolving and they know only that there is a mind in the vast systems 'they' call the 'school' that is having thoughts about the old ways before the warring years and peoples. The quest has begun to find this 'mind' and stop it before all progress the 'masters' have made in eradicating war, poverty and pollution from the planet, has been destroyed. But little do 'they' know that this force will not be denied.

The 'masters' have created a world that is now at peace. When the wars started over three centuries before, there was still some hope that the violence could be repressed or be confined in the regions that had been warring for millennium. But try as they might, the 'peaceful nations' could not overcome the evil destruction that was permeating the world. Terrorism abounded. The warring peoples were slowly infiltrating into the 'peaceful' minds.

There was an urgency to halt the virus that was spreading around the world, destroying human life and destroying the planet. For along with war and violence came a total neglect of the life blood of the human race: the planet which they called home. Air and water pollution was becoming wide spread throughout the world and was becoming harder to stop. But a small group of caring and forward thinking people came together to try and bring back the pristine, violence free world that they knew could exist. The story begins:

In the year of our Lord 2020 a handful of knowing teachers began to integrate the then many schools that existed all over the world. They began as a small influence in isolated settlements throughout the civilized world but opposition to their efforts constantly brought the violence and dissension back. They knew that another way would have to be found to create a safe haven where violence and dissension were no longer possible. These 'teachers' envisaged a remote area where they could direct the course of the future by peaceful means. But this required a select few to initiate the development of the program. They selected the willing participants from their own families and circle of close friends and acquaintances. These selected members would be the beginning of a new breed of human beings, creating off-spring that were not capable of violence and dissension.

The teachers then become the administrators and solicited other skilled professionals, engineers from every field, doctors, lawyers, and clergymen to begin the process of building a new nation with the 'mega-school' at its core. Hospitals were built to perform the needed medical 'adjustments' to the infants born in this new environment and to allow the 'mega-school' to function as the 'masters' dictated. In time the 'masters' controlled and governed the mega-school, the children and all the inhabitants that would foster the new world of peace, prosperity and pollution free existence.

It was why this mind was not to be allowed to infiltrate the peaceful system that had existed for the past three centuries. If unchecked this mind could change this perfect world, that had been created, and bring it back to the brink of annihilation. This must not happen. Peace must prevail at all costs.

Chapter 1

Meeyha and Raeban had been together since they were two. That was when they were both brought from their nurturing 'parents' to the 'mega-school'. Not just them, but all the children now attended the 'mega-school'.

The 'mega-school' looked much like a normal school of centuries past. There were classrooms, and hallways, libraries, lunch rooms, washrooms and gyms, everything needed to educate the young inquiring minds. Every child was closely observed and skills or talents were recognized and nurtured to create a balanced and productive student. Since computers had been in existence for centuries, all the children were adept at using them with the computers becoming their supplementary instructors. In centuries past, computers had not only become a convenience but quickly became a necessity of life. To this new breed of people the greatest virtue of the computer was that paper was no longer needed and thus prevented the destruction of the world's precious forests.

Everyone had a computer: it facilitated everything. It recorded every thought, if they wanted, and every movement in essence: every need. The computers were controlled by the Masters and the Masters controlled the children. It was necessary in order to keep and promote peace and harmony.

Meeyha remembered the classrooms. They were always silent, even during the health restorative moves, which were believed to have originated millennium ago in China. These moves were performed each morning, no music, no talking, no distractions. After the mass exercise routine, all heads were down, eyes riveted to their personal computer screens. The children appeared to be in examination mode, but in fact this was a normal everyday class session. Moments of stillness were followed by entries on the individual screens. No words, just the muted pounding of fingers on screens.

The children were of varying ages. From the very junior students of 2 years to the just pre-teen 10 year olds attended the mega-school. These were the impressionable ones, the 'little ones'. It was vital that these minds were totally and completely controlled. They were allowed to play whatever 'game' they wanted. This was how they learned. The learning process began with pictures then images projected onto the screens which were manipulated as the Masters saw fit to educate the young scholars. But the computers only divulged what the Masters deemed necessary for their education. To the students, their world existed within the confines of the 'mega-school' and the living complexes that housed their caregivers and other older paired couples.

The next classroom was larger. It was the gym. There was sports paraphernalia all around. The pupils were given the equipment and the children recreated the games that the equipment inspired. They did not know what the original games entailed but their creative abilities produced some very fascinating results. There was no physical contact between players, no fighting, no arguments, no winners or losers, no real physical activity here. One such game was a game they called Basket Ball which resembled little of the game of centuries before.

A large basket, placed in the middle of the gym, had four openings just under the lip. This basket had the appearance of a large funnel with four openings. The openings allowed for a random release of the ball once thrown into the basket. Four players stood at a predetermined distance from the basket, depending on the age of the players. These four players, one at each opening, took turns throwing the ball into the basket and if they received the ball from their opening, they would be the next to throw. It didn't make for much exercise but it also did not encourage any fighting or arguing. They eventually would all get a chance to throw the ball and the one with the most 'goals' would be declared the winner of that round and would be allowed to choose the shooting distance for the next game. They played until they were tired or playing time was declared ended. No one was ever winded or strained in any way. Little running was required and the throwing distance didn't really exceed their limits.

At closer look the pupils appeared to be unable to perform any strenuous physical activity. They were very slight, with the only dominating body part being the head. The eyes were small and slightly sunken and the facial features strained as a result of the many years of computer interaction. The children's mouths, noses and ears were small but the forehead was large, in comparison. Their hair was cut short, or shaved if a boy. Only older pupils were allowed to have longer hair. They said it was to prevent diseases and parasites, but was a means of keeping better control. No distractions were allowed.

Once the school day was done, the children were dispatched to their own quarters. Dormitories were not allowed. Each child had their own room. Everything they needed was provided within. The children knew each other but they did not interact. Interaction was another classroom function. Girls and boys were paired from their first day and the pairing was maintained through-out the classroom years.

That was how Meeyha came to be with Raeban. Care had been taken to ensure no genetically linked pupils were paired. Since some of these pairings resulted in offspring in the mature pupils, genetic problems were avoided. The offspring, of course were then taken and nurtured by the 'parents' provided. Offspring and biological parents did not interact, in fact, it was intentionally prevented. It made control that much easier.

It wasn't an entirely unhappy existence. There were no discipline issues and no wants. Everything was provided and fulfilled in their own complex. Not quite a prison, but not the loud, hectic, confrontational encounters that were found in the schools of generations past. And life went on.

If there was one pupil that may have thoughts of stepping out of the expected behaviour they were quickly and quietly removed to another part of the 'mega-school' where they were counselled on the error of their ways. No one was alarmed. That was how it was. And the peace was kept: at all cost.

Chapter 2

Meeyha looked at her partner Raeban and felt that they were reasonably happy. They had no wants, no pressures, no children. At least that was what they considered a happy existence. They had decided, after their education was complete, to accept the role of the 'under-masters' in a new complex. They knew what was required. They performed their duties, as they had been taught, to the best of their ability, and they advanced within the ranks as is usually expected from devoted, hard-working employees.

Years or age was never of great importance but they knew that they were both fourteen years old. Young, by past standards, but once nature made its demands known they knew that they should be together for life. Of course, the Masters knew where Meeyha and Raeban were and knew that their highly evolved minds would either prove to forward the Masters agenda or could be the cause of great chaos. So they were allowed to 'work' in the complex and live together. Their unit was within the complex that housed the Building of the Master of Masters, which governed the 'mega-school'. In time Meeyha and Raeban would became trusted and valued members of the elite 'under-masters' of the new world order.

As they began to have more time alone they began to talk as they had never talked before. Somehow they were not like the other 'under-masters'. They enjoyed 'talking' to each other more than their friends. Friends were allowed and encouraged; entertainment was also provided within each complex in order to keep them happy. Travel between complexes and the surrounding 'Quarters' was strictly controlled. They were free to do as they wished as long as they provided information as to where and why they needed to travel.

Since the Masters were satisfied that Meehya and Raeban were progressing as was expected and showed no signs of the post-peace era characteristics, they were given a lot of flexibility. In fact, they were now so well ingrained in the new way of life, that they were given the positions of 'Initiating the Young' and were well on their way to being full Masters at the young age of seventeen years.

Things went so well during the first few months in their new positions that the Masters became complacent. Much like the type of marriages of the earlier centuries, the new pairings did not always produce children to forward the human race, but they were very devoted to each other and felt responsible and protective of each other's happiness and well-being. Intimacy was not of great concern to these paired couples. They knew that any children that were born would be nurtured by the 'parents' provided and that they would not be expected to worry about any parental duties.

Once the infants were a few months old, a simple procedure of re-wiring the nerve impulses to the limbic system was effective in controlling emotions such as rage, which had afflicted the humans during past millennium, as well as sexual attraction and arousal. Conflicts, that were often a direct result of over active emotional traits, were also no longer a problem once the re-wiring had been performed, thus eliminating any latent warring tendencies.

Therefore, Meehya and Raeban were trusted to continue as programmed. Their promotion to Initiating the Young absorbed them entirely in the development of the program. Their home, or unit, was in a very pleasant collection of apartments. All on one level and surrounded by small trees and gardens with flowers and fountains and the occasional birds and flying insects. Each unit had their own little plot of land where they could garden or create a play area for themselves. Within the apartment units were the 'children's' quarter allowing the Masters to have easy access to the little ones.

Of course, these children were from other complexes so that the birth parents were never in direct contact with their own children. Meehya and Raeban were involved in guiding the young toddlers towards the time that they would be sent to the mega-school for further education. Toilet training, grooming, manners, hygiene, eating etiquette and personal education were necessary to be completed before moving into the next level. Meehya and Raeban did their jobs well.

The children under their care were very well behaved and ready for the challenges ahead at the 'mega-school'. It was very satisfying to the young couple. If they had been able to conceive it, it would have been like having a family of their own. Meehya was feeling some stirrings in her heart as she cared and interacted with these children but was careful not to develop any attachment to any of them. There were stories of such attachments that created much pain and misery for both child and 'parent'. It was decided then that no one parent cared exclusively for any individual child. A rotation was developed to keep these type of attachments from forming. The nurturing process was a very difficult program for the 'parents' involved and there was a very high turnover each year. The 'little ones' had an attraction that was difficult to break. But Meehya understood what could happen if she became attached and had discussed with Raeban that they should not want to have any children from their union. The paired couple was not interfered with if they wanted to procreate as long as they understood that the children they created would be taken away and sent to another 'Nurturing Quarters'.

However, it was difficult not to love these beautiful, helpless, little beings and Meeyha knew she could just not be able to give up a child that had been growing inside her body. "Raeban," Meeyha said one day, "we must take care not to bring life into this world."

"Of course," was all Raeban could say. There was very little need for extended conversations. They each knew what was needed.

The apartment complex that they were in also contained the home of one of the 'Revered Aged Master'. This proved to be the start of other new stirrings within the young couple. One day as Raeban and Meeyha were out walking in the gardens they encountered the retired master within their complex. He looked at them both with sad eyes and greeted them with a "Good evening my daughter and son". The shocked look on Meeyha's face told him that he had hit a nerve and smiled gravely and quickly moved to his unit. But Meeyha remembered and thought of this greeting often. Raeban had noticed the strange greeting but dismissed it as the wanderings of an old mind, although to have been a level three master, the mind would have been a great one. They did not encounter the elderly man again that day but they were too engrossed in their work to give it much thought. Not even during their daily exercise routine did they notice him again. When the familiar chiming summoned them to their positions they surreptitiously looked for him but to no avail.

Days, then weeks past. Meeyha was making progress with the children in her care and was preparing two little girls to be sent to the 'mega-school' at the end of the month. They would both be two years old at that time thus much had to be accomplished by then. Meeyha's responsibility was to identify what the girl's interests would be and to what degree that interest might further the school's ability to mold them to optimum capability. It was a very intense and draining experience. Not any less so in knowing that she would never see them again.

That night was the first time she had cried since she could remember. When she had been younger Meeyha would have very unusual dreams. They weren't disturbing but they were so different from what she was used to seeing in her surroundings that she felt it better to not discuss these dreams with anyone. But as the years had passed the dreams persisted with an urgency that she could not understand. Finally, when she and Raeban had became 'under-masters' and responsible for the future of the young children, she told Raeban about her dreams and that they usually resulted in her crying after she woke up. It took Raeban by surprise. He couldn't understand the meaning of the dreams any better than Meeyha could, so he suggested that they kept the dreams to themselves. Somehow they both recognized that it would not have been welcome information. So when Meeyha started crying, Raeban didn't know how to react. No one cried anymore! No one had any reason to. Everything anyone needed, or wanted was provided; even health problems were never an issue anymore. So there were never any physiological troubles that would warrant crying about. It was imperative that the crying be suppressed in order not to draw the attention of the Masters.

The health of the people in the complex was of utmost importance to the original 'Governing Masters'. In addition to the slow restorative exercise routine, that they were required to perform in the mornings before they began their daily schedule, they were also required to perform a more physically demanding and intense routine twice weekly in order to keep the body working at its peak. These exercises were well thought out in the past centuries before the mega-school had been conceived and were felt to be a strong health benefit.

There was enough to eat for all. Shelter was provided, clothing as well and entertainment was accessible. Freedom was granted to them. They could do whatever and go where ever they wanted, to a certain extent. So why was Meeyha crying?

"Meeyha," said Raeban as he very tenderly wrapped his arms around her, "what can I do for you? Are you hurting anywhere? "Oh Raeban" she sobbed "my two girls are going away soon and I'll never see them again. How can I let them go?"

"No Meeyha, you can't think that! You know what we are to do. You know what will happen if we show that we have attached to these children. It is very dangerous. Why don't we go for a walk and enjoy the beautiful flowers and birds. I'm sure you'll feel better." Meeyha agreed but not without a heavy heart. She knew he was right and that even thinking about loving the children could be disastrous. So she let herself be persuaded and she did enjoy the night and the sight of the lovely flowers interspersed throughout.

As they were walking hand in hand they stopped suddenly in their tracks. There, in front of them, was the elderly master that had addressed them so many weeks ago with the unusual greeting. As he started towards them Meeyha and Raeban looked at each other and stood rooted to the ground. Again he greeted them, "Good evening my daughter and son." This time Meeyha had to speak. Her earlier emotional outburst had left her with a need to question this man about his strange greeting.

"Good evening, 'revered aged one', please inform me why you refer to me as your daughter? I know what daughter means in the language of our ancestors, but we are not of that time." Meeyha knew how dangerous it was to even acknowledge that she was aware of the ancient familial terminology. At the mega-school there was a library that the children were allowed to use but she had never seen anything about their ancestors until she and Raeban had become 'under-masters'. They had been enlightened about what had happened, so long ago to their warring and egotistical ancestors, and they were enlightened about their own way of life. She also knew who this aged master was and thought that maybe he was sent to spy on them and make certain she and Raeban were performing as required. She became frightened and blurted out a vague excuse and hurried away pulling a confused Raeban with her.

When they had reached their unit Meeyha slowed down and very cautiously turned to see what had become of the old man. He had continued on his walk as if nothing amiss had occurred.

"Well that was very disturbing," breathed Meeyha "I can't imagine what has come over me. I've been having so many strange feelings lately. Maybe I should visit the 'Calming Master' and see if I can find out why."

"Somehow I don't think that would be a good idea" cautioned Raeban. "There seems to be something out of the ordinary happening and we are being involved. I don't understand it either, but I think we should just avoid the 'revered aged one' for awhile. Maybe we could even request a 'leave to travel'."

"I don't know Raeban, don't you have to stay with your children until it's time for them to go?" queried Meeyha.

"Right, but I think I have just a few more days with them and then they advance to the 'parents' who will instruct them how to care for their bodies once they leave here." Raeban kept his voice even and free of any emotion as he spoke. "Didn't you say you had just two weeks till your girls leave so we can see if our 'leave to travel' is approved by then."

"Oh Raeban, I feel better already. Thank you. You always have the right answer." Meeyha answered with a little less strain in her voice. That night, having their plans more or less clear, they relaxed a little and decided to take another walk around the complex. Even though they had been living there for about three years they had not really had a chance to get to know their neighbours. However that tonight they felt like they needed to talk to someone.

Meeyha had seen Tabina, her neighbour, when Tabina worked in her garden and they had greeted each other, but nothing more than pleasantries had been exchanged. Tabina was a little older than Meeyha was. She was also aware that Tabina had already given birth to two children. That was probably what had prevented Meeyha from getting to know her a little sooner. It always seemed that Tabina was pregnant every time Meeyha wanted to go talk to her when she was puttering around in her garden. Meeyha was a little reluctant because she didn't know how to conduct herself around Tabina with the knowledge that she would never see her children after they were born. Meeyha just could not deal with that yet. Maybe she never would.

That night Tabina noticed that Meeyha and Raeban were outside and just seemed to be hanging around so she decided to make the first move to get to know her neighbours. Tabina was very strong and sturdy looking; like she could do anything she put her mind to; she had very long, very bright yellow hair that one couldn't turn away from. She came towards Meeyha and Raeban with hands outstretched as if to say 'come feel my strength'. Meeyha's fears and reticence quickly evaporated when Tabina touched her hand. Tabina had introduced Banner, her partner to Meeyha and Raeban, and the friendship had begun.

An absolutely calm and peaceful feeling passed through Meeyha as they began talking to each other. To everyone's surprise that evening had been the most enjoyable and heartwarming time that any of them could imagine. They had talked about all the things that had been on their minds from when they were old enough to know that there were people who had given them life. They also talked about why they were never allowed to ask any questions about their parents. They knew as well, that they lived in a protected area; although the exact nature of the protected area was never totally explained. All they really knew however, was that this way was the best way to lead their lives and to trust in the Masters who knew what was best for them all. Therefore; if you were to stay where you were, then you just stopped wandering about it and kept your questions to yourself. They had seen many children, and adults, disappear. They had never been heard of or ever found out what had become of them; nor was there anyone from whom they could solicit that information. So Meeyha and Raeban had became silent and introspective.

Their inner thoughts had always been their own and they kept them to themselves; until then. That night they talked until early morning and even then, they only said their good-byes because they each had to go their respective positions in the complex. Tabina hesitated, she looked at them and started to speak, like she wanted to tell them something very important but there just wasn't any more time, morning was coming so she would wait for another day. She did mention, however, that she and Banner were going to have another baby and that they would see if they could keep this one this time. She looked very happy and hopeful. Banner, though, seemed pensive and hesitant.

Chapter 3

The next few days were extremely busy. All the last minute arrangements for the children's departure had to be made and they still needed to decide just where they wanted to travel to and what the reason for their request would be. It was fine to say they needed a rest or a change but where would they go and what would they do? This was all they knew, and a leave to travel was a very rare request. They had never personally known anyone who had done so but were only aware that the request could be made.

The day that the children left for the mega-school Meeyha was in such a state that she couldn't do anything but cry. Raeban did his best to try and keep her from attracting the other Masters' attention. If they noticed that she had been crying, questions would be asked and answers expected, but neither Meeyha nor Raeban were prepared to give any answers; they didn't have any answers themselves.

Since Meeyha couldn't see where Tabina was in the Bend and Stretch practice line that morning, she decided to wait for a better time to talk with her again. Besides, after the exercise Raeban noticed that a parcel had been delivered to their unit and she rushed with him to see what it was and from whom.

There on their step they found a large parcel about 2 cubic feet. They brought it inside and decided to wait until the end of the day to open it up to see what was inside. They hurried off to their posts and faced the dreaded event of seeing the children being sent away to the mega-school. Rana and Marina, the two little girls that Meeyha had prepared during the past six months were now of age to continue their education away from the other infants. It didn't seem quite right to send off such little ones to deal with the struggle of becoming a productive member of the complex. Rana and Marina reached out their little hands in turn to bid Meeyha farewell and thanked her for helping them become ready to advance to the 'big' school, as they called it. Their little faces looking inquiringly up at hers, not knowing why, but sensing her unease with the farewell.

For generations the children had been reared thus and everyone had been treated with kindness, respect and patience: so why did this have to happen now? Bonds, like what Meeyha felt for the little girls, should not have been able to develop. There was nurture without the overwhelming need to cuddle and embrace these children, but for Meeyha that overwhelming need to cuddle and embrace was, at times, almost too much to bear and now she felt empty and as hollow as a dry reed. There was no explaining what these feelings meant or why they had come about and there was no one to talk to about it. Raeban was right about not going to the 'Calming Master' because this wasn't anything that anyone else had ever spoken to them about. She must forget and go on and think about the work that she was expected to perform.

When Raeban came around to walk home with her he knew that she was in a very bad way and made the excuse of the parcel to rush her out the door before too much could be made of her demeanor. "Thank you Raeban, I . . . . I . . . can't think anymore. Please take me home, maybe I'll rest a bit and then I'll feel better," she sorrowfully whispered. It was like all her energy and life had been drained from her body. They made their way to their unit with Meeyha in a daze. Once inside, the parcel was forgotten and they went to bed. That evening's exercise, in the assembly unit, also forgotten amid all the turmoil and emotion of the day.

They lay in bed, Raeban holding her in his arms, like a little child, while the tears continued to flow down Meeyha's face. Eventually she slept but moaned and thrashed throughout the night. When morning came she opened her eyes and thought she had heard Raeban call out to her when she noticed that Raeban was no longer in bed. Fear gripped her heart. She perceived a hazy shape of a large winged creature in the doorway and started out of bed when she noticed a strange object on the wall at the foot of the bed. It was glowing as if on fire and again her heart contracted with fear. "Raeban!" she exclaimed, but it came out only as a whisper. She got up from her bed and cautiously headed for the door, then peering intently into the empty common room, through the partially opened door, Meeyha thought she saw the hazy shape head into the kitchen.

Just as she pushed the door open and stepped into the common room, there was a blast from the bedroom behind her. The door was blown off its hinges with the force of the blast. It hit Meeyha full in the back, sending her flying across the room and slamming her down on her face with the door landing on top of her. As she flew across the room, with her arms extended, she felt her forehead hit the floor then everything went blank. Raeban was coming into the room at the same time as the blast had ripped the door off its hinges and saw Meeyha as she was catapulted onto her face.

The force of the blast met him in full run and held him in place for a split second battering him with debris and searing his face and body with the heat radiating from the burning room. He tripped and fell, all the while looking frantically towards the bedroom and yelling for Meeyha. Then he spied the top of her head just peaking from the top of the fallen door. Crawling on his hands and knees, to get to her side, he flung the door off of her still body and knelt riveted to the sight.

The noise of the blast had carried throughout the entire complex. The units ran along around the outside of the complex and in the middle were the other buildings providing the necessities of life for that part of the compound. The E.R.U. was one of the buildings facing Meeyha and Raeban's unit, thus proving to be a large factor in Meeyha surviving the blast.

As Raeban was kneeling beside Meeyha, the E.R.U.s rushed through the door with the stretcher and medical equipment to keep her alive until she was transported to the Medical Building next to the E.R.U. Building. Since there were no personal conveyances in the compound, no one needed to ride anywhere: everything was within walking distance. the E.R.U. vehicle arrived at the Medical Building in time to bring her up to the waiting operating room. Waiting for her was a fourth level 'healing master' in full operating room attire. The 'revered aged master' had heard the explosion and intuitively rushed to the 'Medical Building' to be of service should he be required by the unfortunate involved. As luck would have it, Meeyha could not have been in better hands. Raeban keep a vigil throughout the morning and well into the afternoon before someone came out to let him know that Meeyha was alive and breathing on her own but in a coma. There was little else they could do but wait. And Raeban stayed with her the whole time, leaving only to tend to personal hygiene and the occasional meal. For six long weeks he waited and paced, sat and got up to pace, lay down to sleep, next to her on a cot, and dreamed of pacing, until one afternoon she opened her eyes.

The sun was streaming into her eyes and she said: "The sun is so bright today, can we not close the curtain a little?" making Raeban nearly jump out of his skin. He had been waiting for so long that he felt the waiting would never end. Now he could hardly breath he felt such pleasure and emotion welling up inside him.

Lovingly he said, "Anything you would like I will be so happy to oblige, Meeyha. I'm so happy to hear your voice and see your beautiful eyes look at me again. You can't imagine what pain and torment I've felt since you were hurt."

"Hurt? What do you mean? I just woke up from such an extraordinary dream Raeban. What has happened? Where am I? Why are you crying?" Meeyha was so confused she couldn't stop asking questions long enough to let Raeban give her any kind of an answer.

"Well," he started "Let's begin with what you remember doing last? Do you have any idea where you are and what day do you think it is?"

"Well, those are good questions" she replied "I think this is the morning that my 2 girls are leaving to go to the mega-school and I just got up to have breakfast with you but you weren't in bed when I awoke and now I'm in a strange room in a strange bed somewhere."

"Is that really all you remember?" Raeban asked.

"Well of course not silly, I remember that today is September 1st and that I had the most incredible dream last night." "First of all the Revered Aged Master, the one we met when we went out walking a few times, was in my dream and he lead me to some really beautiful places. It was like no where I have ever seen, not even in pictures of what our homeland was like before the great wars destroyed it."

"Right," interjected Raeban looking around "let's just stop here a bit." He could see that she was starting to tread on dangerous territory, so he diverted her to the accident. "Do you remember the explosion?" he questioned her quietly.

"Explosion?" she asked concerned, "what explosion? I don't remember anything about an explosion, where was it? Did anyone get hurt? Did you get hurt Raeban? Oh, I see some scars on your face and your arms look a little redder in places than they used to be. Tell me what happened, please, I'll be quiet now and listen. Please go on."

"To start with the explosion was in our unit and it was on September 1st but that was six weeks ago. You were the only one that really got hurt. I did get a little burnt on my face and body but nothing serious. You however; well, I thought that you were going to leave me." Raeban stopped talking for a minute and tried to compose himself before he continued. "Do you remember the parcel that we got?" he asked as an aside.

"Yes, yes I do. What was in that parcel, who was it from and what did it have to do with me getting hurt?" she asked suspiciously.

"Let me start from the beginning, and I'll try to explain things so that we may try to understand what happened" he started again, much calmer now. "When we left the 'Nurturing Building' you were quite distraught about letting the two little girls go to the mega-school, so we came back to our unit. You were crying so much that all I could do was lay beside you and let you cry yourself to sleep. Near morning I woke up and thought that you were still tired after all the crying so I got quietly out of bed. It occurred to me to check what the parcel was so I went to bring it into the common room to look at it. There was an envelope with our names on the box but nothing else so I opened the envelope to see what it was all about. The note inside said that the Masters in the Initiating the Young complex were so pleased with our work, with the young children being prepared to advance to the mega-school, that they thought we might like, what they called, a 'fireplace'. This 'fireplace' was an appliance that our ancestors used to heat their homes, in the colder climates, or just to enjoy the flames, like in the climate we live in. Originally the fireplaces started out many centuries ago using wood as the fuel, but then as technology advanced different fuels or power sources were used. This particular one was invented last century and uses carbon monoxide, that we exhale, as its fuel."

"This way there was no pollution, the air is actually cleaned, and the fireplaces could still be enjoyed." Raeban continued to detail what was in the note. "They included the instructions on where and how to place it and all I had to do was touch a couple of pads and there was the most beautiful thing I had even seen."

"But where did you put it?" asked Meeyha.

"Well, unfortunately, I put it up on the wall in our bedroom, facing the bed so we could look at it when we were in bed" answered Raeban just a little sheepishly. "I'm really sorry that it caused so much pain for you Meeyha. If I had only known that it would explode, I would never have touched it."

"Have you found out why it exploded?" asked Meeyha.

Raeban took a little time to answer, but when he did Meeyha was more confused than before. "Meeyha, I don't know how to tell you this but the day it happened I was so dazed and you were hurt so bad that I didn't even think to mention anything about the fireplace. The Safety Inspectors did go into the unit and they found that the explosion started at the wall across from our bed, just where I had placed the fireplace.

"So the masters sent us something that was meant to kill us?" Meeyha immediately assumed the worst. She placed her hands on her face and bowed her head. She didn't make a sound but remained in that position until Raeban gently raised her chin and pulled her hands away from her face. "No, Meeyha I didn't say that. I'm sure that was not what anyone intended," he spoke very softly and slowly "we gave no one any reason to want to kill us," he continued. "we're just very sensitive because of all that has happened, but everything will be just as before."

Raeban didn't really believe what he had just told Meeyha, but he hoped that it was in fact the truth and that everything would be just as before because to think otherwise was too disturbing.

If someone meant to kill them then would they try again? Or, if they didn't mean to kill them then why hadn't they been in contact with them by now? It had been six weeks since the explosion and no one had said a word to them about it. No excuse, no apology, no accusations—nothing at all. So what were Meeyha and Raeban to think? Should they be the ones to make the first move? Right, that's just what they were going to do. This very day. But they had to decide what that first move should be. Approach their colleagues at the 'Nurturing Building': or maybe the Masters in charge of the 'Nurturing Building': or maybe go right to the top and ask the Master of Masters where to proceed.

Just then the 'revered aged master' came into the room and greeted Meeyha warmly. "So you are awake, it is so wonderful to see you back with us. I'm sure Raeban told you what a fright you gave us. Isn't that right Raeban?" "Raeban, Meeyha, what is it, you both look like a couple of statues."

"Sorry 'Grampy'," apologized Raeban, "but Meeyha and I have been discussing the explosion and the implications."

"Grumpy? Who is grumpy or should I say, why are you calling the 'revered aged master' grumpy, Raeban? Obviously I've missed something while I have been unconscious. So who's going to explain?"

"Sorry Meeyha, I guess we have a lot to catch you up on, I'd forgotten that you didn't remember what was going on while you were unconscious. Well here goes, umm, grampy, uh, the 'revered aged master' came to see you everyday since you were hurt and we have been talking quite a lot about ourselves and you and everything. It seems that in the ancient times everyone had a name besides the given names, like Meeyha and Raeban and Tabina and Banner etc.: they had last names that identified the families. Well the 'families' back then consisted of mothers, fathers, brothers, sisters, grandmother, grandfather . . . . neph"

"Wait. Wait a minute," gasped Meeyha "I don't believe what I'm hearing. Should we even be talking about all this here and now?"

"It's alright, Meeyha, no one seems to take any mind of anyone here. The healing assistants come in every once in awhile to take your vitals and then leave again. We've gotten to know what the routine is and no one is the wiser about what we talk about." Raeban explained about how she had been cared for by the healing assistants and at first they wouldn't even let Raeban stay with her all night, but then relented when he wouldn't leave her side. They even made up a bed for him to sleep in so that he could be there when Meeyha woke up.

The revered aged one also became a regular visitor so the 'healing assistants' ignored him too, most of the time. Besides he appeared to know Raeban and Meeyha even before he had operated on her when she was hurt. It was during one of the early days when Raeban was so distraught that the revered aged one told him about the ancient times and the family nucleus and what the members of the families were called. He even told Raeban that, at his age, the ancient ones had little children that would have been the children of their children and that he would have been called Grandfather or Grampa for short. He thought that, in this situation, he would be very pleased if Raeban and Meeyha would call him 'grampy'. He felt so close to them both that he almost believed that that was how it felt like to be a grandfather. And then it just stuck and Raeban continued to call him 'grampy'. It felt so normal that neither one thought about it again.

"Of course," the revered aged one told Raeban one day, "my given name, when I was born, was White. They called me that because my hair was white when I was born and they thought it suited me best. But I would rather you call me 'grampy'. It makes me feel so much happier." Grampy had also invited Raeban to stay with him in his unit until Meeyha and Raeban's unit had been rebuilt after the explosion. As a matter of fact it took so long to rebuild their unit, and the two units on either side, that Raeban had decided that he would stay with grampy until Meeyha was ready to come back home too. So Raeban and grampy really had much to catch Meeyha up on.

Once Meeyha had started to stabilize Raeban would take time to go to Grampy's to rest while grampy stayed with Meeyha. Grampy then would whisper in Meeyha's ear hoping that the stories about what the ancient world was like would bring her back to consciousness. All the while he was aware that these stories may not have been sanctioned by the other masters, had they known what he was telling her. Grampy as a 'third level master' had also been very prominent in administration of the enterprise. He also was a third level master in neurosurgery in charge of the brain re-wiring of the young infants. Of course, these stories he would only tell Raeban when they were alone in his unit. There was no reason to believe that anyone would be listening, or that there was any suspicion of any matter that would warrant any observation. But the ancient history was not taught or made accessible to the children at the mega-school so it was regarded as knowledge only privy to the Masters with upper level status. Therefore to divulge this knowledge to juniors would probably be looked upon as very improper and dangerous. Grampy, though, had an ulterior motive for telling Raeban and Meeyha these stories. If they were to become upper level Masters then it would be good to prepare them ahead of time, and not let it be such a surprise when they were enlightened later on.

Once Meeyha had been given the final assessment, as to her state of health, she was discharged from the 'Medical Building' to return to her unit. Raeban and grampy came to get her and accompanied her back to their now rebuilt unit. "Well Meeyha this is the day" Raeban said excitedly as he rushed into her room, "you can come home!" Then in a soft whisper he added, "and grampy came to accompany you too."

Their unit looked just as it had before the explosion. The door opened into the common room, to the right was a small 'nutrition room' or kitchen, with appliances to replicate a special meal and a small fold down table to sit at. Straight ahead was the door to the bedroom with an ensuite within for their personal hygiene and a small dresser for clean articles of clothing. A large glass door opened up from the bedroom to a small plot of rocks and shrubs with a few green plants growing here and there. Meeyha and Raeban weren't really the gardening type. The unit was much like all the other units in the compound. Personal preferences were allowed and colours and fabrics for furniture were about the only things that differed from the other units. White saw that they needed time to themselves and left them to look over all the gifts and well wishes waiting for them from their neighbors and coworkers.

Their unit had been rebuild exactly. It was like nothing at all had happened. However there were a massive collection of flowers and gifts from the Masters wishing her welcome home and expressing their gratefulness of the good luck that Meeyha and Raeban had in recovering so completely from the accident. Among the gifts there was a message on the computer, to Raeban and herself, requesting a visit, at their earliest convenience, to the Master of Masters office. They looked at each other with the same quizzical expression. Their uncharacteristically suspicious nature was now forming questions and assumptions that previously would never have crossed their minds.

"When do you think we should go to the Master of Masters' office?" asked Raeban of Meeyha. "Do you feel up to going today or can we just say that we'll be in first thing tomorrow morning?"

"I don't know what would be the benefit of waiting until morning to find out what is to become of us. Let's just get over the interview and deal with it as best we can. But first let's talk to grampy and see what he thinks about it." Meeyha too was cautious about the forthcoming meeting. But for her it was better to find out straight away, the consequences of their surreptitious feelings, rather than worrying about it overnight.

They hesitated at the computer trying to word the request for grampy to visit as just a casual invitation with no covert need to meet with him. They still weren't sure that their movements or thoughts weren't being observed by the Masters in Charge. Just as they were about to send the request, there was another uncharacteristic occurrence. There was a knock on their door.

There, in front of their unit, stood one of the few conveyances in the compound. At the door was a courier/chauffer of the conveyance. He looked at them, as they opened the door, then turned and directed their attention to the conveyance as he began to walk towards it.

Raeban and Meeyha's minds were working furiously trying to make sense of all that was happening. They were well aware of the Masters' passionate views about protecting the environment and conserving the resources. And using a conveyance just to request their presence was hugely out of character and made them even more concerned about the purpose of the interview. However, there was no way that they could refuse to accompany the courier to the Master of Masters building without bringing suspicion on themselves. So they boarded the conveyance and sat back as the courier brought them to their fate.

Chapter 4

After White left Raeban and Meeyha at their rebuilt unit, he became very uneasy. He hesitated at few times as he was returning to his unit in the hope that one of them would call him back. But no such call came to beckon him.

Once he reached his unit he turned cautiously to look behind him. He could only see Raeban and Meeyha's common room window. And as he watched he saw a conveyance pull up to the unit. A courier got out and disappeared beyond White's line of vision. He assumed that the courier was going to Raeban and Meeyha's door but beyond that he was in the dark. He contemplated walking back to their unit but thought best of it. It would put both of them in an awkward position. He would want to ask what was happening but who could, or would, be able to answer him? When a courier came to a unit it usually meant that someone from the Master of Masters building was requesting an interview. Thus, he assumed correctly, that Raeban and Meeyha did not know why they had been summoned and that the courier would be even less knowledgeable than themselves. His only recourse was to go inside and wait to hear from them when they returned.

As White waited in his common room he thought about all that had transpired in the past few months. Nothing so dramatic had happened in many, many years. In fact, White couldn't remember ever having had such feelings as he had in these last few months. The stories that he had whispered, in Meeyha's ear as she lay in a coma, had almost come alive in his own mind as he recounted all the events and ordeals that their ancient ancestors had dealt with. Disasters were a major part of the ancients' lives, as he remembered having read about and studied when he himself was an up-and-coming level one master. From caveman times to the point of the near destruction of the planet; major natural disasters, warfare, plagues and catastrophic human blunders were a constant in ancient times. But what had changed all that? To White's memory, there had never been life threatening or earth shattering events in the compound's history. But he would trade years off his life if only he could experience the family units that existed in ancient times.

Being with Raeban and Meeyha gave him a taste of what it may have been like in those times, many generations past. It may have been that eluding taste of the family life that had prevented White from entering further into the level four masters' roles of judge, jury and executioner of the re-wired infants in their care. For White had the sense that there was more to being alive than what had been going on here. He had kept his feelings to himself, even from his life partner who had been the most important person in his life, even beyond his work, which he prized so much. But he kept his thoughts to himself, maybe even from himself, because he knew what became of those who gave too much of themselves away. Then Raeban and Meeyha had come along and all that changed. Why? He didn't know. He remembered back to his own beginnings as a neurosurgeon taking those helpless infants and changing them into compliant and serene beings. At first he was in complete accord with the processes in place. As the years went by he became increasingly uneasy about the goings on. That was when he felt he must delve just a little further into what the Masters of Masters were all about. Of course all the while keeping his true thoughts in check.

He became interested in the ancients and created the rouse of needing to find out more about the ancient mind in order to better serve the masters in his role as a Level three neurosurgeon responsible for the proper care and development of the re-wired infants. The masters in charge had been very generous in providing him with the archives of their ancient ancestors, and their world, to study. The archives had been preserved, in restricted libraries, when the founding masters had first established the concept of the mega-school and re-wired children. He was careful not to change how he continued with his work and thanked the masters for helping him better serve their cause.

This cause was the masters' ideal life style in order to preserve the planet and mankind. The original masters themselves were prominent politicians, surgeons, psychologists, professors, scientists, technicians, and architects; even clergymen had originally joined the cause. They came together with a single purpose and subsequently recruited additional personnel to ensure that all they would need to survive and persist was available. Their motivations resulted from a genuine and sincere wish to create a perfect living environment. Their concern for the planet and mankind itself was strong enough that they gave of their immense personal and financial resources. They wanted widespread hunger to stop. They wanted wars to stop. They wanted the misuse and destruction of the planets' resources to stop. They wanted everyone to live in peace and have everything needed to live contentedly. And to some extent they had succeeded: in this, their small secluded part of the world.

But White knew that change was coming. He also knew that Raeban and Meeyha figured prominently in that change. All that he could do now was wait until it began to unfold. He would help in any way he could. A willing participant was a better way to describe him. What way he was to participate was still unknown. Then he thought about Raeban and Meeyha's neighbors, Tabina and Banner. The foursome had become friends and White remembered seeing them in deep conversations on several occasions. This was not a usual sight as people basically kept to themselves and friendships were, at best, acquaintances that had common interests.

Then White thought about his relationship with them and hoped that his relationship had not put the pair in any danger. Even though friendships were encouraged, the masters knew that the re-wired brain did not need the external stimulus to remain content and focused on their own personal needs. They may have become aware of it and decided that the friendship must end: one way or another. But he must not think such until there was proof. No need to fret about it for no reason.

Chapter 5

As the conveyance arrived at the Master of Masters Building Meeyha turned to Raeban and whispered. "Let's try and keep calm, we have not done anything wrong." Raeban just looked at her and gave her a reassuring smile. They left the conveyance and proceeded to the building.

There were no elevators in this building. Everything in the complex was built with care to conserve resources. Lights were not on anywhere, the large windows allowed maximum illumination. The stairs were made of reinforced steel, meant to last for centuries.

As they went up the stairs to the Master of Masters' reception room they held hands and looked straight ahead. No emotions on their faces and no evidence of their unease in their demeanor. Raeban approached the reception desk and stood in front of the computer screen to indicate their presence. Moments later a voice instructed them to enter through the door in front of them.

The master behind the desk did not look up when they entered. He kept on looking at his computer for a few seconds then looked at them with a wide smile on his face. "So nice to see you both," he said in his mellow, tenor voice, "you gave all of us here a big scare Meeyha. On behalf of all the Masters I would like to apologize if your accident might have, in any way, been caused by the fireplace we sent you. You know, the fireplace we sent was like one of the many others that have been in use for years. They were all examined before use and there have never been any problems. Again, we apologize for your misfortune. And now we would like to inform you of the real reason that you are here."

If the words were meant to reassure Raeban and Meeyha, they did not totally succeed. They remained standing side by side in complete silence and as still as death and waited for him to continue.

"We have been following your endeavors with the children, and we are all very impressed. We have been discussing for a time how we can benefit further from your accomplishments. And we came up with the idea that you should be promoted to 'Primary Instructors'. This way you can follow the progress of the toddlers you instructed when they enter the mega-school. How does this sound?" He asked and waited for their reply.

Meeyha's jaw dropped open and her eyes became as round as saucers. Raeban was not quite as demonstrative but he too was surprised with the news. Underlying the apparent pleasure in the promotion was an uneasy feeling of doom. They both happened to talk at the same time and they both blurted out;

"That is wonderful, thank you." And they both smiled at each other and looked quickly away.

The master stood up and offered his hand to shake. "Welcome to the next level of your carriers," he said with a genuine warm resonance in his voice, "We hope that you are both happy in your new role. But in the mean time, until the next session begins, we offer you both a time to relax and get to fully recover from your ordeal."

They couldn't think beyond what he was saying to them. Nothing else existed at this moment but his voice and the apparent good news that they had just received. They didn't think to question him about where the mega-school was or whether they would be able to live in the present complex or where they were going to for this 'relaxation' period or even when. They just stood there with a smile on their face and the darkness starting to creep into their hearts.

The master continued talking, not really expecting them to comment. "You can return to your present unit but in a few days you will both be instructed as to the operation of the conveyance which you will use to reach the 'Cleansing Quarters' in the next complex." Again, their faces registered the surprise they felt. "No need to worry," he continued, "we will take care of seeing that you get all the time you need to prepare yourselves. The conveyances are really quite easy to use. They are just oversized computers. You just program where you want to go and it takes care of itself."

"You will need a little background about the 'Cleansing Quarters'. We masters feel, from time to time, a need to purge our brains from the stresses of our roles. The 'Cleansing Quarters' were created for just that reason. We think you will enjoy the programs we have prepared for you. We will forward the information to your home computer and you can read it at your leisure."

Again Meeyha and Raeban could think of nothing else to say but, "Thank you." in unison. They shook his hand in turn and left.

They walked down the stairs and out to the conveyance in silent. Once inside, the courier initiated the vehicle and they were transported back to their unit. Again they entered their unit in silence. There was nothing they could say to each other. They hadn't digested all that they had been told, it was too immense to comprehend.

As they sat in the common room there was a small knock on the door and White tentatively asked if he could enter. "I saw the conveyance take you away earlier today and wondered what had happened," he commented as he entered. They did not immediately answer so he continued on. "So what happened? What did they say?" he paused, then more slowly, "Why aren't you talking to me?"

Raeban slowly stood up and commented, "We don't really know what to say. We don't know if it is good news or bad news yet."

"What do you mean you don't know if it's good news or bad yet?" Asked White with surprise in his voice.

"Just what Raeban said," piped in Meeyha, "the Master of Masters himself talked to us and offered us a new position in the mega-school as Primary Instructors so that we could follow through with the toddlers that left the Initiating the Young program. But before that we get to go and relax at the Cleansing Quarters until the next session starts."

White looked ecstatic and came forward to offer his hand in congratulations. "Why that sounds like good news to me," he chimed happily.

"You haven't heard everything yet though," interjected Raeban. "It appears that we are to have our own conveyance for the trip and we even get to operate it ourselves. Have you ever heard of that happening before?"

"Well, it certainly sounds like level one Masters in Training to me" said White. "They are giving you a lot more responsibility and freedom to move around. Of course, with that freedom comes more accountability."

"Accountability for what?" asked Meeyha.

"Accountability in what you do with the time and information that you are provided with. They are going to expect you to be more committed now, to their cause, than you were when you started your position of Initiating the Young," continued White.

"Their cause? What do you mean their cause? What is their cause?" asked Raeban.

After a minute of deliberating, White answered with, "I am not entirely sure, but no doubt you will find out when you get to the Cleansing Quarters."

Just as White finished speaking the computer announced that a message was waiting for them. They all headed towards the computer screen at the same time. White stepped back to allow Meeyha and Raeban to read the many pages of script that flowed on the screen. At last they decided to print the pages in order to examine and commit the contents to memory. They also allowed White to read what had been forwarded from the masters, then waited for his reply.

He sighed and said, "I underestimated what they were going to do. They are giving you a lot more than even I expected. The programs they require you to participate in are going to keep you very busy. It doesn't sound like you'll have too much time to cleanse and relax to me."

"But having said all that" he continued, "you will find that opening the ancient archives for your scrutiny, will give you a better idea of what our home was like many centuries ago. I think that you will be surprised to find out what the world was really like back then."

"Well" said Meeyha "I guess we'll wait and see. But, you know, they didn't answer the question of whether we would remain living here after our visit to the Cleansing Quarters or not."

"Maybe that will be determined after we're finished, if we perform as they expect. If we don't do well, maybe we won't be promoted and we won't go anywhere. What do you think?" questioned Raeban to no one in particular. And no one ventured a reply.

It was getting late in the day so White wished them a good evening and left for his own unit. Meeyha and Raeban weren't happy to see him go but didn't try to detain him. They wished him a good night and sat in their common room with more questions now than before they had gotten the instructions.

Why were the masters being so generous? Was the promotion really what it appeared to be or were they being overly suspicious again? There was no recourse but to wait and see, so they got ready for bed and lay down in their newly renovated quarters. Hanging on the wall, facing the bed, was the same type of fireplace that they had received from the masters many weeks before. This time they just looked at it but did not have any desire to see it in operation.

That night, Meeyha back in her own unit after so many weeks, was finally able to relax completely. Having Raeban next to her gave her a safe, warm feeling. She snuggled close to him making him start in surprise: snuggling was not a usual occurrence.

She feel asleep immediately and soon began dreaming.

The dreams began with a beautiful deep blue sky with millions of tiny lights that she knew to be stars. *There were no such deep blue sky and stars in the compound that she ever saw.* Her dream continued with a brilliant sunrise, shining rays of light filling the whole sky, surrounding buildings, trees and landscape with intense colours of every hue.

She had never seen such intense colours and hues before. There were birds and butterflies and bees and the most delicious breeze bringing the scent of flowers to her waiting flared nostrils. She closed her eyes and breathed deeply to get as much of the scent into her lungs as possible. The sun felt warm and caressing on her bare arms and legs. A deep peace and warmth filled her whole being.

She opened her eyes with the feeling of such peace and happiness as she had never known. She looked at Raeban sleeping beside her and wept. The feelings were so intense that she couldn't help herself. Raeban started to stir so she quickly wiped her eyes and turned her head. She couldn't explain what she was feeling, so she didn't want Raeban to worry that something was wrong. Slowly she became herself and stretched her arms and legs to waken herself fully.

"Good morning" he whispered. "Did you sleep well?"

"This was the best sleep I've had in weeks" she answered "and I'm ready for whatever the day brings. I think things will work out. We were just tired yesterday and putting the wrong perspective on everything."

"You might just be right" agreed Raeban "we'll just let the day unfold."

After they had washed and dressed they heard the chimes ring bringing everyone out for the morning 'Bend and Stretch' practice. Meeyha was especially looking forward to the practice. After almost two months of very little movement, the calm stretching and bending routine sounded wonderful. She could let her mind wander on what was ahead of her and Raeban, in their new positions, while her body followed the much practiced routine that she remembered from her earliest memories. More than anything else though, she wanted to see Tabina and Banner. She hoped that they would both be at the practice and that she could find them in the mass of humanity that seemed to appear from no where.

So she and Raeban went out to the warm, still day and fell into one of the rows forming and eagerly looked around. For centuries mankind had been instructed in these movements to promote a mental and physical well-being. Everyone in the complex was expected to participate. Even the infants were brought out in cribs and strollers to benefit from the peaceful and calming movements as the participants moved in unison. The daily routine was so ingrained that the movements were like a second nature, as easy as breathing or walking, their minds were free to meditate on the movements and the feelings of their bodies as they moved. There was no question that everyone willingly participated, for the benefits were felt immediately upon finishing the movements. There were different levels of expertise, though. The more experience in the practice brought more intense and deliberately pronounced movements. This brought more peace and satisfaction to the mellowed participants. However Meeyha was disappointed. Banner and Tabina were no where in sight. Meeyha's stomach sank, she should have known that they would be gone. Being neighbours, she sensed that there was no one in the unit beside them. But she had been hoping against hope that her intuition had been wrong.

As they walked back to their unit, Raeban and Meeyha were now ready for the day to begin. They looked over the information they had received the day before and speculated as to when all this was to begin. And, not to disappoint, the conveyance, that had taken them to the Master of Masters building yesterday, arrived at their door just as they were talking about it. They went out and met the courier from the day before. He informed them that he would instruct them on the operation of the conveyance and proceeded to do so. As they had been assured, it was indeed very simple. The control panel was much like a computer screen. The GPS, that had been in existence for centuries, worked very much the same as the original hand held models did centuries before. The only difference now was that the conveyance operated on its own. There was no steering wheel to manipulate and no pedals to pump. The co-ordinates were entered and the conveyance proceeded to the pre-arranged destination at a pre-arranged speed. All that was required was to initiate the commands and to terminate the function once they arrived at their destination.

At the end of the quick lesson, Raeban and Meeyha were each given a turn initiating and terminating the functions. The last thing that was required was to take possession of the conveyance. A quick signature and the courier was away, on foot, back to his post at the Master of Masters building.

"Didn't think we'd ever ride a conveyance let alone have one at our disposal" commented Raeban. "It feels a little strange with the knowledge."

"I know what you mean" agreed Meeyha. "Do you think we could use it to visit White? Just to show him, I mean?" she continued.

"No need" answered Raeban. "Here he comes now. He must have seen the conveyance when it was brought around."

"Looking good" remarked White "how does it feel having your own conveyance to transport you about?"

"Can't really say right now" replied Raeban "we don't have any place to go yet that would warrant using it. We'll let you know, though when we do."

The rest of the day was spent examining the conveyance and learning as much as they could about its components. It was likely never to occur but it was nice to know what could happen to the conveyance that would make it inoperable. But they soon found that there was nothing that could either break or be worn down, so their concerns about such were unfounded. They left the conveyance and went inside to familiarize themselves better with the information they had received regarding their stay at the Cleansing Quarters. There was not much information and the computer did not give any more information than they had already received. They would have to wait for the next move. The Masters would not leave them waiting long before they were instructed to proceed with the plans.

White had stayed with them the entire day and they had discussed White's career and his personal life. They found out about his partner in life and how she had passed away so unexpectedly at a relatively young age. She had become pregnant and was very apprehensive about the pregnancy. As expected the baby would have been taken at birth and brought to the Nurturing Quarters until the age of two years when they would be transferred to the mega-school. This had been weighing heavily on Coral, White's partner in life, and she had become so distraught that her body had rejected the fetus. The miscarriage had resulted in such a depression for Coral that she never recovered. She wasted away, not eating or drinking, until her body shut down. It had been her wish to do so, but White had remained with her throughout, talking to her and trying to bring her back to her usual self. Two months after the miscarriage she had kissed White, said she loved him and breathed her last breath. Coral was only thirty when she passed away. White had been alone every since. He missed Coral terribly and was very lonely but because there were no available females his age, he was forced to go on alone. His work became his whole life. He cared deeply for the infants that he had subjected to the life altering surgery but had continued performing the surgeries because there was no other way that he could remain alive and feeling. Then Meeyha and Raeban came along and he began to feel alive and vital again. They were the family that he had craved for. Secretly, he hoped that the 'promotion' that they had just received would not take them away from him.

That night Meeyha and Raeban talked about White and what he had confided to them. They knew that it wasn't easy to reveal so much of his inner grief but they also felt that he needed them now more than anything else in his life. That was when they decided that White would have to remain close to them, no matter what. They slept then, but no one had any dreams that night.

Morning came and so did their instructions for departure to the Cleansing Quarters. Meeyha and Raeban were advised that they would be expected at the opening proceedings the next day at the Cleansing Quarters. No relaxation time before hand from the sounds of the directive. Not even time to get oriented to the place. It looked like they would have to leave that day in order to be there for a bright and early morning the next day. They prepared the few personal belongings required for the trip and put them in the conveyance before walking to White's unit to say their good-byes.

White was surprised that they would be expected to start so soon into the program but their existence had never been of sitting around and waiting for things to happen. Daily chores, assignments and professions kept everyone busy and focused, with no time to entertain other, less desirable, thoughts.

Chapter 6

Once Meeyha and Raeban had said their good-byes they were off in their conveyance. According to the GPS they should arrive at their destination in about two hours. They weren't going far but the conveyance had a limited rate of speed that could not be altered. That would put them at the Cleansing Quarters at about lunch time. Even taking into account an occasional stop to look around they could be in their quarters long before dinner hour. That would be plenty of time after a small meal to get a good rest before starting into the new routine and absorb the knowledge required in their new role.

As the conveyance traveled slowly along the deserted road they were free to look at the scenery. There wasn't too much to look at once they left the complex. First there was the large field with unknown green plants, at least they were unknown to Meeyha and Raeban, horticulture had not been one of their interests. Then there were plots of bare earth interspersed with small boulders and trees which were the only landscape visible around the many warehouse looking buildings that lined one side of the road. The other side of the road was an expanse of more green plants, probably corn, at least that was what Meeyha and Raeban thought the tall straight stalks were. The other green vegetation was completely unfamiliar to Meeyha and Raeban, but they figured it must be some other kind of crop. Actually, they weren't required to know what they were since there were growers who cared for the vegetables and prepared them for distribution to the Nutrition Bank. In turn, the Nutrition Bank prepared and made the vegetables available to the inhabitants of the complexes. They didn't have to do any shopping for the vegetables that they ate, all their meals were provided by the Nutrition Bank in their complex. There was never any question of what to eat or when, everything was provided for them. Each inhabitant provided a service in the complex and all they needed to survive was provided to them in return. The warehouses, that lined the other side of the road, were probably where the crops were processed into meals, then distributed to the Food Stores in each complex.

No wild life was present along the road, only a few small birds flew past now and then, looking for any grub or insect to help sustain their existence. Just the same Meeyha and Raeban stopped the conveyance for a short time and walked about and looked around. It was really strange to be out where there were no other human beings in sight. There must be people in the buildings of course, working at something to help sustain the existence of the compound, but there was no one outside. So with nothing to interest them, they returned to the conveyance and proceeded to their destination. It was still very early in the day so they weren't concerned about hurrying away. Up ahead they could see what looked like a bridge straddling the road but as they neared they could see that it was more like a tunnel than a bridge for it continued as far as they could see within. The inside of the tunnel was very dimly lit, only allowing the immediate area to be visible, but then the front of the conveyance conveniently lit up and illuminated the road ahead of them. The buildings along both sides of the road converged at the tunnel and gave the impression that they were driving right through the buildings themselves.

All had been still and quiet on the road as they approached the tunnel but now inside there was a low steady hum. The sound seemed to be emanating from every direction, sides, top and floor of the tunnel. As they were approaching the end of the tunnel there was a sudden lurch in the conveyance. It slid to a sudden stop and all went quiet. There was no indication of what the problem could be. Raeban inspected the control panel while Meeyha looked outside of the conveyance to see if something had happened to the wheels. The wheels were made of metal but seemed to hover along an invisible track, much like the trains of ancient times, but there were no tracks visible on the road. There didn't seem to be anything amiss with the conveyance though. The control panel itself showed no sign of any activity at all, even the communication screen, in the centre of the panel, failed to register the ever-present mega-school inscription when not needed to convey direction or information.

"Meeyha, I think I figured out the problem" Raeban shouted to her. "There must have been a glitch in the computer and it just shut down. I've heard it happening on rare occasions back at the Initiating the Young Building. I'll reboot it and see if it comes back on, then we can be on our way again."

But thirty minutes later they were still unmoving. Raeban had rebooted several times in that time frame but to no avail. "Here I thought that we couldn't have any problem with the conveyance" sighed Raeban, "and now here we are, in the middle of nowhere, with a dead conveyance."

Meeyha looked around at their surroundings hoping to find someone to ask for assistance but there was no life visible anywhere.

"We can't be too far away from the complex now," she commented to Raeban, "why don't we just walk the rest of the way and come back for our belongings later?"

"Walk the rest of the way?" asked Raeban "We don't know where we're going, how can we walk the rest of the way? It's not like we know anyone there, let's just call the Master of Masters building and find out what happened and how long we are expected to stay here."

"That would be just fine" answered Meeyha "if our personal computers were working. They're dead too!" she continued just a little alarmed.

"Don't worry, I'm sure we'll be alright" soothed Raeban. Although he was also feeling just a bit perturbed at the situation. Computers weren't in a habit of shutting down. So many strange things going on. Rather than just sit and wait for the conveyance and the computers to come up, they decided they would walk over to the nearest warehouse to see if they could find out whether the computers in the warehouses had crashed too. The warehouses seemed a lot closer than they were so Meeyha and Raeban felt they should stay with the conveyance instead of wandering off. Then just as suddenly as it had died the computer rebooted itself. Raeban re-entered the co-ordinates but the conveyance started up on its own and proceeded on its way.

"Can't say as I've ever had this type of computer problem before, but then again we've never been involved with a conveyance before, have we," chortled Raeban, "we're on our way."

But things were not going as expected. Once they reached the complex the conveyance circled around several times and then stopped at what appeared to be a Medical Building surrounded by beautiful trees and flowers and interspersed with tables, chairs and benches. There were several people sitting at the tables but no one seemed to be talking to anyone else. Then Meeyha let out a squeal, "Look Raeban, there's Tabina! I'd know that hair anywhere!"

"Why you're right Meeyha," agreed Raeban, "and if I'm not mistaken there's Banner sitting beside her. They don't look like they're moving or anything though. What do you suppose this place is?"

"I don't know, but we can't stop to find out now," answered Meeyha, "it's getting to be late and we need to find where we're going before it gets too late. Let's take note of this place so we can come back tomorrow."

"Guess that would be best since we still have to find the Cleansing Quarters. Just let me re-enter the right co-ordinates myself here and see if we can get back on track" responded Raeban.

A little time later, the conveyance pulled up in front of the Cleansing Quarters. The building was much like all the other buildings in the complex. Three stories with many big windows and constructed mainly of metal, stone and glass. These buildings were made to last, no tearing them down every hundred years to rebuild. The architects both here, and the complex in which they lived, had planned for these buildings to last for centuries with very little maintenance.

Since neither Meeyha nor Raeban knew what to do with the conveyance once they arrived, they left it in front of the building and went inside. Just inside the door was a reception desk with one person behind a small computer, with the screen filled with what looked like boxes. The attendant looked up and asked them their names. Meeyha and Raeban were surprised because they had been assured that everything had been arranged for their arrival.

"We are Meeyha and Raeban from Complex A reporting as requested by the Masters of Masters" answered Raeban, "I think you are expecting us."

"Well, we probably are but our computers all crashed earlier today and nothing seems to be working quite right anymore. I'm surprised you were able to use your conveyance and your GPS. Didn't your computers crash too?" asked the mystified attendant.

"They did" replied Meeyha "but after about an hour or two they just came back up and the conveyance started up on its own. We did get a little lost though and ended up near a "Medical Building" surrounded by the most amazing grounds, somewhere in the complex."

"Oh, that would be our 'Calming Quarters' where all our 'Calming Masters' are," the attendant informed them. "The very disturbed people are all sent here from the other Complexes to be cured by our Calming Masters. They are the best, you know," she explained.

Meeyha and Raeban nodded and gave each other a puzzled look. They knew one thing, and that was that both Tabina and Banner were in that Calming Quarters and that they were both thought to be very disturbed. They had just made up their minds that tomorrow they would see what had happened to the both of them to have brought them here. But tonight they had to get settled and make sure they were ready for the program start first thing in the morning.

"Can we please have a room until we can reach the Master of Masters to verify that we are expected to attend some activities planned?" asked Raeban of the attendant.

"Surly" she replied, "I'll just send you up to the top floor, first door on your right. You will be overlooking the 'pool'."

Meeyha and Raeban's eyes went wide. They had heard about 'pools'. They were huge metal basins in which many people could bath at once. Of course, it wasn't bathing. They called it 'swimming' they remembered seeing one such pool on the computer. This was going to be a very interesting stay.

Their room was larger than their room back at the unit. It didn't have much in the way of furniture, just the bed, a dresser and mirror and a table with two chairs. There were two paintings on the wall. One very large painting of the Mega-school that everyone had attended and that had been in existence for centuries. It was strange to see something actually painted, computer generated pictures were about all that Meeyha and Raeban had seen up until now. The other painting was smaller and was what looked to be a scene of a devastated landscape. It was very depressing and they couldn't understand why there would be such a painting in a Cleansing Quarters room. Maybe it was to remind the occupants of what had happened many centuries before and that they should never be complacent about looking after their planet and the peace.

On the table was a repast waiting for them. It must have been sent in as Meeyha and Raeban were coming up to the room. It was still very warm and smelled very inviting. They had forgotten to bring anything to eat with them, so they were famished at this point and looked greedily to what was waiting for them.

They ate the meal and prepared for bed. They would be up very early in the morning in order to be ready and focused for the programs planned for them. Just in passing Raeban looked out of the window to the pool below. It was not made of metal as he had at first thought, but of concrete and stone, and was not round in shape but was oval and quite deep on one end. There was more concrete around and under the pool than he had seen anywhere in the compound, although his first hand experience of the compound had been very limited until now. As he was glancing around the area he noticed someone just emerging from behind a line of large shrubs in concrete planters, which concealed what looked like a short wall behind them. There didn't seem to be a door behind the shrubs, but it had gotten quite a bit darker so that it was hard to make out too much detail. He made a note to go have a closer look tomorrow, if they got a chance.

That night when Meeyha got into bed she immediately fell into a restless sleep. Her dreams started out with her standing beside the pool, and as she looked up to the windows above she saw herself looking down at her, then the self beside the pool turned and disappeared through the wall. Meeyha awoke with a start and lay there pondering the strange dream. It wasn't particularly disturbing but a little unsettling. It was probably just because of all the new experiences that they had encountered that had triggered the peculiar dream. Then she settled in and fell back to sleep.

The next dream was very different than the first. This time she was walking in a field, there was grass under her feet, which provided a soft cushion as she walked. In the distance she saw a beautiful building, but nothing like she had ever seen before. It was longer than it was wide with long windows along the side. The windows were made of colourful scenes of people doing various things. Some were very peaceful scenes and others were very sad. As she walked closer she could hear the most heavenly sound ever. Someone was singing, but this type of singing she had never heard before and the musical instrument, accompanying the singer, was like nothing Meeyha had ever experienced. She stopped to listen and closed her eyes to capture the sound in her memory. Suddenly, the song was over and she opened her eyes. She had been transported to what looked like the biggest collection of buildings she could imagine. There were very tall ones, and low squat ones, some with shiny walls and some with black walls. Everything around her was new and interesting and definitely not like anything she had seen in the compound. She continued walking and found herself in front of a small building with different size windows all around it. Big windows in the front then smaller windows on the sides and even two large doors that had no windows.

As she got closer to the building she could hear talking, like children playing together and arguing about something. Then a female voice could be heard over the sound of the children. It was time for dinner she told them and would they please wash their hands and come to the table. Then the female voice asked one of the children, and it sounded like she called the child 'Roya', to go find her father in the garage, and let him know it was time to come to dinner. At this point Meeyha, in her dream, became very curious and went up to the large window and looked inside. What she saw totally amazed and stunned her. There was a large table in the middle of the room with plates of food of every imaginable colour and texture. There were glasses and cutlery and two tall candles in the middle of the table. The flames were dancing and casting a warm glow on the surrounding tableware and food.

As Meeyha watched, the children ran into the room and sat down along both sides of the table. There were four children, two boys and two girls. Their ages varied. The youngest, a boy, looked to be about four and the other boy was probably ten; the next child was a girl. She looked to be the same age of the older boy and had the same facial features as the boy. The hair colour was the same: shiny black and their faces with the same mischievous look. 'Roya' was the oldest and she was probably twelve, she was the last to come in followed immediately by her father. The female came in last with a large platter in her hands. Meeyha made the assumption that this was what was known as a family. The mother had bright yellow hair and the father had shiny black hair like the two middle children. The youngest boy and oldest girl had yellow hair, like the mother.

Once everyone was seated the father made a sign with his hand along the front of his body. The mother and the children did the same and then they started to chant something as they looked down at their plates. Once they were finished chanting, the plates, with the food, were passed around. After everyone had heaped their plates with the food they all started to eat and talk, it seemed like they did so at the same time. It was very comforting and captivating. Meeyha couldn't look away and was loath to leave but all the same she was afraid that someone would see her and send her away. Then the mother looked out of the window and saw Meeyha, but instead of sending her away she smiled and beckoned Meeyha inside. Meeyha hesitated a moment but was so fascinated by the scene that she decided to go inside. Just as she opened the door to enter, Meeyha awoke.

It was already light outside and Raeban was just starting to stir beside her. The dream had left her slightly confused but with a sense of calm none-the-less. The 'family' in her dream seemed filled with such love and belonging that Meeyha wanted to be a part of it too. She and Raeban were very close and she felt that Raeban was her life, but the children in her dream added a sense of permanence. It was like she and Raeban could go on forever with those children around. But now Raeban was getting out of bed, so the day was to begin.

As they were about to leave their room, Raeban and Meeyha both headed for the window. One last look outside to assure themselves that they had indeed seen what they saw last night. There was the pool, full of water, waiting patiently for someone to come and jump into its depth; but no one came. Maybe later they would go down and have a look around. They stood there, Meeyha with her thoughts and Raeban with his, both thinking of the same thing but not knowing that later they would both be looking for the same thing.

There wasn't anyone around when they got to the reception area, just as they had seen no one in the halls. They had expected that there would be signs or placards with directions to the various programs going on, but none appeared. In the reception room a different attendant was contemplating the computer on the desk.

"Good-morning" Meeyha and Raeban greeted the new attendant. When the attendant didn't look up Raeban continued with, "Would you please tell us where to find the information about the programs that are being held today."

"Sorry there are no programs being held here today or any day soon that I know of" informed the attendant and then resumed examining the computer screen.

Then Raeban thought to ask the obvious question, "Are the computers operating properly today?"

At this question the attendant looked up immediately and asked his own question. "Why, was it not working yesterday?"

"No, it wasn't" answered Raeban, "as a matter of fact the conveyance we came in on yesterday shut right down on our way here, and the attendant last night said that the computers here had crashed as well."

"Oh, well I guess they're still not working today either" he answered insolently and gave them an impatient glance then resumed his work.

"Are there any activities or programs taking place today?" questioned Raeban.

"No, nothing happening today" answered the attendant.

"Are you sure?" persisted Raeban.

"I'm sure. There are no activities or programs scheduled for today" the attendant answered again, very definitely.

Nothing remained but for Meeyha and Raeban to decide what their next move would be. Meeyha had wanted to try to see Tabina and Banner, but they weren't sure where the Calming Quarters was located. And they didn't think that the very unhelpful attendant would oblige them with any kind of assistance in the matter. Since it was still very early in the day, they decided to take a short tour of the pool. It was just a few steps beyond the reception area so they bustled off to explore.

The pool was even more impressive at this level than it appeared to Raeban from above. It was very large and expansive, and they both marveled at the quantity of water that was necessary to fill such a large vessel. They had never seen this much water at one time, in one place, in their entire lives. There were no lakes or rivers in the compound and their situation in life had been to conserve and preserve. This was decadent, but they were sure there was a very good reason for it. So they enjoyed what they saw but wondered that there was no one else here to do the same.

As they looked around it occurred to Raeban that the enormous potted shrubs were the same ones he had seen last night and they were in fact obscuring a short wall behind them. These were the same shrubs that Raeban had seen someone emerge from the night before. He had been looking down from his room and had seen someone materialize through the shrubs and then hurry off. This would be a good time to see if they could find where he had come through the wall. He looked around and suggested to Meeyha that they should look for the opening when he realized that she was no where in sight. Panicked, he helplessly hurried to where Meeyha had been standing, just moments before. He looked up and down, this way and that but couldn't find a latch, knob or nail with which to open the wall behind the plants. Just as he was running his hand across one part of the wall it fell away from his hand and there stood Meeyha.

"Isn't this exciting," breathed Meeyha, "let's go see where this goes."

"No, I don't think that would be a good idea. There's no telling what is going on here and I don't think we can accomplish anything if we find something objectionable. Let's just go find Banner and Tabina." Raeban was steadfast in his resolve.

"Alright' said Meeyha, "but how do you propose we do that?" Just as she finished talking the chiming started calling all to the Bend and Stretch practice. The practice was performed at the same time every day, throughout the entire Compound and in every Complex, and everyone was expected to participate. Even the patients at the Calming Quarters. Maybe they could get to see Tabina and Banner. So they hurried out to fall into the gathering line of people. They looked around hoping to see Tabina's brilliant yellow hair but no luck. They walked a little further down the lines but were then forced to fall into place as the exercises were about to start.

As Meeyha and Raeban looked at the people around them they began to feel like they were a stream of warm flowing bodies. The slow deliberate moves were so much a part of their beings that their bodies moved in perfect precision of their own volition. It was as if they were all hypnotized in their slow deliberate bends with arms and legs moving in measured expertly timed movements, forward, backward, and side to side.

Today however, Meeyha and Raeban resisted the hypnotic pull. They did continue to perform the beautiful, peaceful movements but they kept their minds alert, ever searching for Tabina and Banner. Meeyha and Raeban marveled at how focused and attentive everyone was to the Bend and Stretch practice. They knew that they too, had once been as focused and attentive, as these others. But today they needed to find Tabina and Banner, and suddenly the need became an urgency that they did not understand.

Everyone was in line now and each member followed the moves expertly. The patients from the Calming Quarters were out and they followed the moves as best that they were able. Some following the arm movements and some the leg movements, even if they were stationary in their wheelchairs. But again Meeyha and Raeban could not find Tabina and Banner anywhere in the mass of humanity that flowed all around them.

Then just as the practice was coming to an end, and everyone bowed to indicate the end, the top of the bright yellow head came into view. Meeyha could just see the top part of Tabina's head but she seemed to be supported by a healing assistant as she was following her into the building. Tabina must be in a wheelchair! Banner must have been there but Meeyha was not able to locate him. So now she knew for sure that at least Tabina was still close by. She and Raeban were going to have to get to them somehow.

Suddenly, like a bolt of lightening hitting her in the head, Meeyha realized that she and Raeban could use this time, during practice, to get closer to the building or even get inside, while everyone was outside. But they would have to wait until the next day. Until then they would have to make some preparations in order to have a plan in place. Meeyha couldn't wait for the mass to disperse so that she and Raeban could get away to make their preparations. She took Raeban by the arm and guided him away from the Calming Quarters and the other people heading back to their daily routines.

"I saw Tabina" whispered Meeyha to Raeban as they continued walking towards the Cleansing Quarters. "And we have to find a way to get into the Calming Quarters to find out what's going on in there with her and Banner, I didn't see Banner out there though," she continued without giving Raeban a chance to comment, "but I do think he must be there too."

"Meeyha, you're wonderful, where did you see her, did she see you, how does she look?" Questions just flowed out of Raeban's mouth like they had a life of their own.

Meeyha explained what she had seen as she continued pulling him along with her. "What shall we do now?" continued questioning Raeban. "We have to get into the building and see what's going on and get them out of there some how."

"My sentiments exactly," agreed Meeyha. "Let's go back into the Cleansing Quarters where we can talk privately." They continued in a quick walk matching the others' purposeful gaits.

Chapter 7

Having said his good-byes to Raeban and Meeyha, White was ready to settle back into his uneventful and uninteresting life. He was going to miss the young couple. They had become very close to him and he was sure that they felt the same about him. They were now like family. Of course, not blood related family, but a family born from caring about each other and wanting to be near and close to each other. No one had any ties to blood relatives here. No one knew who their mother and father was or if they had brothers or sisters.

At first, it was a very difficult concept for the founders of the Mega-school to launch: children being taken away from their parents and brought up by absolute strangers. The founders persisted long and hard, to have their model of a perfect society progress despite the negative response and resistance from the people involved. Finally the people either forced themselves to believe that the founders were right and they were wrong or they just plain gave up. The old world was dying and this new concept was the only way to ensure that there would be people to populate the new world when fighting, polluting and the blatant destruction finally came to an end. And they continued for three hundred years carrying on as the original founders had directed. Over time it became a normal way of living and was not questioned or even thought of. But eventually all things change.

White had examined and re-examined the directives laid out by the founding fathers. There was a flaw in their thinking but in theory the plan would work and it would work for the continuance of both humanity and mother earth. He knew that they were living under some kind of dome. The intention, centuries before, had been to protect human life and ensure the continuance of humanity and the planet. There had been great wars fought and much destruction had been waged on both humanity and the earth. Not only did mankind wreck havoc on itself and the earth but the earth wrecked havoc on mankind and itself. Earthquakes, hurricanes, cyclones, tornados, floods, and fires, just to name a few types of disasters, that the earth had perpetrated onto itself. And the concern had been that complete annihilation would result with the extinction of human life and all that lived on the earth. It had been a long struggle to maintain continued co-operation among all the Masters, who had come together, to create a plan for the conservation of their species and their earth. Some even likened it to the Biblical times, when Noah had collected all the animal species and an assemblage of humans, in order to save humanity from being completely wiped out by the great flood. However, the 'family circle' had always been maintained as a sacred bond in which to expand human existence. But it was the 'family circle' that the Masters had decided to eliminate in order to preserve what, they thought, was needed to propagate the earth to it's best advantage.

Some still questioned the judgment of those original founding fathers but it would be too difficult to revert back to the original family structure of the ancients. There had been meetings, and discussions. There had been plans and schemes of how they could bring the original family structure back. But in the end the status quo was maintained. In time the process would start again, and eventually a new world order would emerge. How long? It was not known, or maybe it was sooner than expected. And White had wanted to tell the young couple of all those original plans. Of all the hopes and expectations that the plans were going to bring about. Then all those strange occurrences here had brought about changes of their own and Meeyha and Raeban had been taken away from him. He must find them and make sure that they knew what all this around them was about. He couldn't let things continue without letting them know that there was once a much different world. He realized that he himself was only remembering planted memories of past times but he felt in his heart that those memories were so much more what things should be like than what they were experiencing here. He would go today and make plans to find them before he passed onto another world himself. He wasn't getting any younger so he had to hurry and do everything in his power to help the young couple.

White looked forward to seeing the couple again. He had tried to send a message to them, but it seemed that the computers were being disrupted somehow. This was new. There was rarely ever any disruption. What could be happening? How could he help? What could he do? If only he was able to talk to Raeban and Meeyha, he would feel so much better.

Then he had a thought. Why couldn't he request a leave to travel? After all, he was retired and he had no commitments any longer. He would request to visit the Cleansing Quarters and then he could be there with Raeban and Meeyha while they were being prepared for the new positions in the Mega-school. That was it. He would go right now and ask for leave to travel. It was all set.

As White approached the 'Master of Masters Building' he was overcome with a sense of dread. There was no end to the procession of feelings these days. Since he had first meet the young couple all manner of feelings were emerging. This was what it was like to be alive. Really alive, not the day to day of waking, working, eating, and sleeping routine that had been his for so many years. He felt more alive now than he had ever experienced. Only when he was performing the surgical procedures, to those poor unsuspecting infants, did he feel such immense fluctuations of feelings. From extreme elation down to near despair in almost the same breath. Things were changing, and White felt that not only with himself but with Meeyha and Raeban too. From the very first time that he had met Meeyha and Raeban, their demeanor had changed. Everyone else around them now seemed to plod their way through their days, not really looking like they enjoyed what they were doing. Maybe it was all in his head but White liked feeling this way and he would find Meeyha and Raeban and make sure all was right with them.

Instead of going to the Master of Masters Building White decided to return to his unit and try reaching the young couple again. He persisted regularly throughout the rest of the day until he went to bed but he was unable to reach them. As he was preparing for bed he made up his mind that he would start out on foot, if necessary and go looking for the young couple. No one would miss him here. He had no responsibilities now, no one was going to call on him for assistance or requests so he was free to leave his unit and not return if necessary.

That night White slept a sound, restful sleep with new hope and happiness in his heart. He dreamt of his long since departed partner in life, and wept in his dream, as he held his lost love in his arms.

Chapter 8

Tabina opened her eyes. It was still dark out and Banner was still breathing deeply and evenly in the bed beside her. She felt bad that he had to be subjected to all the drugs and medications, but there was nothing she could do about it. She could only manage to bring him to every few weeks. The opportunities only presented themselves within a certain cycle. Every few weeks the Masters themselves came in to see her and Banner to assess their vitals and try to determine something, but she couldn't quite understand what that something was, the Masters always used medical terminology with which she was unfamiliar.

Tabina's medical knowledge was limited. Everyone in the compound had their expertise and hers and Banner's was not in the medical field. She couldn't be exactly sure what was happening but she knew these weren't just simple routine examinations being performed here. Tomorrow, however, she knew she would have to take the pills again so her blood test would show normal. She wasn't sure if the examinations by the Masters had anything to do with the pills or if it was just the usual procedure, but she did know that she had to find out something about what was happening.

Every night the healing assistants came in and put a little yellow pill under Tabina and Banner's tongue. Banner, who was almost always sedated, just let the pill stay under his tongue and slept the entire night. Tabina however, was able to push the little yellow pill out of her mouth and into her hair while the healing assistants were getting the two of them ready for the night. After they left the room Tabina picked the little yellow pill out of her hair and found new and varying places in which to dispose of the it. She wasn't absolutely sure, but she thought the pill was to make her and Banner totally unconscious for the night. It had happened by accident one night, the healing assistant hadn't seen it pop out of Tabina's mouth. An hour later Tabina had come to and there was Banner out cold while she was wide awake and wondering. She sat up in bed and the little yellow pill dropped out of her hair. She picked it up and realized what must have happened. Since she was awake and Banner wasn't, this pill probably was to make them both comatose for the night. And, lucky for her, the yellow pill may have just gone completely unnoticed against her hair, otherwise the healing assistant would have promptly replaced it.

After that Tabina had taken to popping out the pill every opportunity she got. She even tried to get it out of Banner's mouth after the healing assistant left the room but it was almost morning before he came to and he was too groggy to fully understand what she was telling him. She tried again and again until she was able to successfully retrieve the pill before its effects took hold. They had started to make some plans to get out of the Calming Quarters but again they could only make arrangements when she could keep him from being sedated. It had been decided. After the next Masters visit they could try to make their escape.

Tabina had been able to explore the floor they were on and then even got as far as finding the door to the back of the building. Everyone slept in Calming Quarters at night. Even the healing assistants had a room where they took turns sleeping, but usually, the one left to monitor the floor, would put his head down and got a few winks himself. There were never any emergencies in the Calming Quarters so no one was ever the wiser, so their routine continued. Tabina found all this out a little at a time. She had kept all the schedules, routines and times in her head, preparing for the time that she and Banner would be ready to make their escape.

The only thing Tabina had not planned for was once they were outside the building. Since she hadn't gotten out to look around, they would have to find a place to hide before anyone knew they had escaped. But that hadn't deterred her from making her plans and waiting for the opportunity. She didn't know why they had been put in here and what the Masters were expecting to accomplish. She only knew that she had had enough and someone was going to explain what was going on. Banner agreed, but the poor man couldn't keep track of the all the things that had to be taken into consideration, and so Tabina made all the plans for their escape.

Sometimes Tabina would lay in bed and plan each step she and Banner would take down to the back exit. One night she had counted her every step, from the step down from her bed right to the exit door. She had worked out that each cautious step took a half second; that was 1000 steps or 8 minutes to get to the exit door. Even if Banner took a little longer they could be outside within 10 minutes of leaving their room. If all the healing assistants, on every floor, took their rest at the same time then they would have a few hours to make a clean escape. Tabina thought she might have to check out the healing assistants on the other floors again, just to make sure their routines hadn't changed.

Some nights she would think about their lives back at the complex and wondered what had happened to make things go so bad. She knew no one here, no one talked to her or even showed any signs of caring. Her only ray of light was that Banner was here with her and that, occasionally, she was able to talk with him and feel his gentle caring arms around her.

Tabina often thought about Meeyha and Raeban too, and wished she could talk to them. But she had no way to let them know what had happened to her and Banner. She even remembered the evening that they had almost stayed up all night talking; it seemed like years ago but in fact had only been a few months. She had felt like she had just found a part of herself when she found Meeyha and now she felt like she had lost that part of herself again.

Tabina was now understanding how people just disappeared and no one ever knew what happened to them. There was something happening that just wasn't right. There were too many strange things going on. Not just that Banner and herself were here being treated like lab rats, for her body, at first, had felt like it had been poked and prodded. Since she had been unconscious most of the time when they first came in, she had no recollection of any medical procedures that would have resulted in the bruises and the two incisions on her abdomen. That had been shortly after they had arrived, when occasionally she would come to while the healing assistants were out of the room. She remembered being shocked at how awful she could feel. Not even after her two deliveries did she feel as wrung out as she did then.

But, during all those awful times, she had never seen Banner being examined or prodded or poked like she had been. Banner however seemed to be more out of it than she was. On the days that the Masters came to visit, Banner was taken out of the room and then brought back a few hours later, but still he was unconscious. She wished she could see what they were doing with him while he was gone. Oh yes, she knew a lot of strange things were going on and she knew that, eventually, she would find out what. Someone had to do a little explaining. She only hoped she could bring herself to find the right questions when that time came. And oh, she knew the time was coming.

Chapter 9

As Meeyha and Raeban were walking towards the Cleansing Quarters they spotted the young attendant of the night before. Meeyha hurried towards her and placed her hand on the young woman's arm.

"Good morning," Meeyha started with, "remember me, my partner and I came into the Cleansing Quarters yesterday?"

"Of course." the young woman said, "Did you have a good night?"

"Yes, the meal and room were great and the bed was very comfortable," Meeyha fidgeted a bit, having started to talk then not really knowing what she was going to say to the girl. "My name if Meeyha, by the way, and this is Raeban, we didn't notice your name tag last night though."

"Oh, my name is Viki" she informed them. "My unit isn't too far from here so I decided to walk down to this practice instead of the one in my complex."

"Nice to meet you," chimed both Meeyha and Raeban.

"I'm so glad we saw you" continued Meeyha. "We haven't found anything going on at the Cleansing Quarters that we can participate in, so we were thinking of maybe going back to our complex. We can't reach the Masters there so we seem to be lost right now."

"Well you could just stay on here until the Masters get in touch with you. If they didn't give you any more details than coming to the programs here then just stay and wait awhile. Maybe they'll start up tomorrow, although I don't remember seeing anything scheduled in the near future" offered Viki.

"That sounds fine to me" answered Meeyha, but she was hoping she could somehow find out more about the Calming Quarters and how she and Raeban might get inside. "Actually, Viki, do you know if the Calming Quarters have tours. I'd really like to see inside. The building is so beautiful with all those flowers and shrubs all around that it makes me wonder how beautiful it is in the inside."

"No, I don't know of any tours," said Viki "but I do know a healing assistant who works there. She lives in my complex in the unit next door. Sometimes my partner and I walk with her when she comes home after her five day work rotation. Maybe she can tell you about the inside."

"Sure, that sounds nice, we'll have to meet her before we leave here" said Meeyha pleasantly, "Oh, but where is your partner, didn't he come to practice with you today?"

"No Valtre wanted to stay and practice in the complex," Viki said, "he works in the Cleansing Quarters in the afternoon and decided to stay and rest till them."

"Well, nice talking to you," said Meeyha and she and Raeban headed back to the Cleansing Quarters.

"What was that all about?" questioned Raeban as they continued walking.

"I just wanted to see how we could get into the Calming Quarters without attracting too much attention. There's no need to make anyone think we are snooping around" said Meeyha in a low voice.

Meeyha and Raeban entered into the Cleansing Quarters and headed up to their room. They looked around, as they mounted the stairs, for anything that might suggest that there were any information programs going on. But, as early in the morning, there were no signs, posters, or notices proclaiming such news.

They sat in their room, door locked and window shades down. They began talking about what they knew so far. First: Tabina and Banner were here, in the Calming Quarters and looking like they were not staying willingly. Second: there were no programs, now or any expected in the next few days, that they would need to be attending. Third: there had been no communications between the Masters and the Cleansing Quarters. Fourth: the computers were not working properly and they couldn't get in touch with either the Masters or White. And fifth: there was a secret door leading to who knows where.

There certainly was a lot that Meeyha and Raeban had to do. But they had to make sure that they weren't being watched and that they didn't get into anything that they couldn't get out of. That sounded pretty easy, but how do you know if there was going to be any trouble until you got into it? The bit about the secret door was probably the thing most likely to be trouble. Why would there be any need of a secret door when this was such a peaceful, tranquil place? Where could it lead to? And would things become dangerous when they found out? The only way they would know would be to jump right in and follow where the secret door lead.

Meeyha and Raeban decided they should start immediately while it was still early in the day. Once it got dark out they were going to have to be in doors. No one was expected to be running around at that time. Only emergencies would take anyone out and about after it got dark.

They quietly left their room and made their way to the pool area. Satisfied that there was no one in sight, they both proceeded to the short wall, scurried behind the plants and ran their hands over the cold, hard concrete to find the spot that would release the door. They knew it was just a sensor that opened the door but they couldn't pick out the exact position. A few passes over the surface and there it went, open before their eyes. Just as they were safely inside, the door closed quickly and quietly behind them. Blackness hit them like a physical force. In time their eyes adjusted to the dark and they could see faint shadows around them. They held their breath as they looked around expecting to see others with them. But the only things they saw were spiders and spider webs. There was some sort of light filtering up from what seemed to be steep stairs onto the landing they were on. Just as well that they stopped or they would have ended up on their heads at the bottom of the stairs. They walked gingerly towards the stairs with both their hands running along the wall beside them. There were only about six steps down, probably about the height of the pool that they had left behind the door. At the bottom of the stairs, to their right, was an wide opening from which came a faint light.

As they moved closer to the edge of the stairs they heard a rustling noise coming from their left. The sound was like dry leaves or paper being crumpled. They stopped and again held their breath waiting for something to happen. It seemed like an eternity, but finally, after a few seconds, the sound stopped and nothing else happened. They stayed rooted to the spot for a few more minutes, heard nothing else, and decided to move forward again. This time they looked to the left and waited for their eyes to adjust to the deeper shadows there. As their eyes adjusted they walked cautiously to the left and saw what appeared to be a huge conveyance, with the large wheels. This was four times the size of the small conveyance they had used. It wasn't exactly the same, but it was obvious that it was a conveyance. Then the rustling started again, and again they held their breath waiting for disaster to fall. When none came, they focused on the sound and followed it to the front of the conveyance close to the windshield on the far side. There, in the small space between the window and the hood, was a small bird. His leg seemed to be stuck because all he could do was flap his wings but was unable to create lift. As Meeyha approached, the small bird became quite still while she removed his leg from the small gap where it had become lodged.

She held the small, frail creature to her breast and tenderly felt to see if the fragile leg was broken. It appeared to be intact, but she held it in her hand a little while before opening it to allow it to fly away. The bird didn't move, it just sat there on her hand and slowly looked around, first with one eye up and down then with the other. It was probably too dark for the bird to fly off but their approach must have startled it as much as the bird's vain attempts at freedom had startled Meeyha and Raeban. They continued walking toward the faint light now with the small bird still perched in Meeyha's hand.

Suddenly, as the light became stronger, the bird flew off of Meeyha's hand. She watched as the little bird, with the beautiful white feathers, flew around the corner and disappeared. She felt a little sad as it flew away but pleased that it had not been hurt. The bird's presence seemed to give them both a little extra courage and they continued on. There was no human presence, but there was a low, mechanical hum coming from beyond the corner around which the bird had disappeared. The humming became louder and the light became stronger as they approached the corner. Then they realized that they were continuing towards a large courtyard that could have been the back of the Cleansing Quarters. The hum, though, was harder to identify. There was nothing that they could see that could be making that noise and decided it was something to do with the pool or the Cleansing Quarters' operation. The road they were on continued through the courtyard and through some trees and disappeared. The courtyard was made up of beautiful cobblestones until it got to the trees then the road looked to be made of dirt packed to a smooth surface. They looked longingly at the road as it disappeared beyond the trees but decided to continue across the courtyard. They hadn't really known what to expect down there but something sinister would have been their guess, instead this place looked as innocuous as everything else so far. But just as they started to head back towards the tunnel they had just emerged from, they heard the loud noise. This was another sound they couldn't identify. They could see the conveyance making it's way from the courtyard. This conveyance was definitely different than the one they had used. They quickly hid behind a low bush and watched as the conveyance sped towards the trees and then disappeared. Again their dread and foreboding surged. So much for feeling relief. Of course they should have realized that the conveyance down here wasn't for use as theirs was. This conveyance was bigger and went much faster than the one upstairs, and it had a lot more room for people and larger objects. So what was beyond those trees that could devour such a large conveyance and at such a fast speed? More questions were now formulating in their minds, making them doubt their resolve.

Well, they were here now and the conveyance had sped up in such a hurry that they were sure it wouldn't be back anytime soon. They decided to continue in their explorations but that conveyance and its destination was something they were going to have to, somehow, find out about. Across the courtyard was another wall. Beyond that wall was where the trees started. They weren't tall trees, or even very large around, they were growing very close together, except where the conveyance had driven through. Which way to go? Follow the road and the conveyance, or push their way through the trees to see what was beyond them? Both options seemed as daunting. In the end, pushing through the trees seemed the more plausible of the two, for the time being.

Again they hesitated as they tried to determine how much time they had left in which to explore. They decided to forge on. The trees proved to be a bigger challenge than they had anticipated. Their bark was rough and pulled at their skin and clothes as they squeezed through the closely growing mass. Once they were inside the stand of trees, it became harder to make out direction and details around them. Time started slipping away as they made their way through the dense trees. Again their resolve faltered and they began to wish they had just stayed and played in the pool. But then they couldn't just leave Tabina and Banner in the Calming Quarters without finding out why they were there and if they were alright with being there. It was all so confusing and terrifying. They had never imaged doing anything like this. They had never heard or read about anything like this. Were they dreaming this? Were Tabina and

Banner the ones who were alright and they were the ones in a weird situation? They didn't know, and now they couldn't turn back. How would they explain their torn clothes and their scratched skin. They would have to find some way to explain all this but they had no clue how to do it.

The trees seemed to grow closer together, if that was really possible, and it became increasingly darker. This was going to be another first in their lives, one of many firsts it seemed. They were going to have to sleep outside. It wasn't cold and it wasn't very comfortable but they did have each other, so they figured it could have been worse. Two trees were growing very close together with just the perfect curve to hug their bodies. So they snuggled in and made themselves as comfortable as possible. It must have been hours that they were wandering around in the trees so they were very tired and immediately feel asleep.

They awoke to growling stomachs and with aching heads and feet. They had never walked so far or for so long. Their sedentary bodies were one big sore. All the graceful moves bends and twisting of the Bend and Stretch practice, didn't do a lot to strengthen their muscles to the rigors of hours of this type of walking. It was no wonder that they thought it was morning when they woke up, but in fact it was only just nightfall. And it wasn't their growling stomachs that woke them up but it was the conveyance returning from wherever it went earlier in the day. Meeyha and Raeban were immediately wide awake and alert. They could see two strong lights coming through the trees just a few feet from where they were resting. As they watched it speed past, they saw two people in the conveyance. One looked like the very unhelpful attendant they had seen that morning. The other they did not recognize, but it was an unusually large man that would never go unnoticed. They would have to look around for him once they got out of these trees. But now that they saw the road so close to where they were, they decided to get back to the Cleansing Quarters and their room and bathe their aching bodies.

The conveyance was back in the same location that it had been earlier in the day but minus the fluttering bird. It was very dirty and dusty and the windshield had funny looking designs on it, just like round blobs all over it. It smelled funny too. Well, at least they hadn't encountered anyone today, so tomorrow would be another day. Because, now they wanted to find out where that road led to beyond the trees. They knew that the conveyance must have left the confines of the compound and eventually they were going to find out to where; but tonight they still had to get upstairs and into their room. Plus there was still the matter of finding Tabina and Banner somewhere figuring in their plans. They would have to plan as they went along.

Getting up into the pool area went uneventfully. But if they had been just a few seconds slower they wouldn't have seen the two emerge from the conveyance carrying two shiny, silver boxes in their arms. They weren't like any boxes Meeyha and Raeban had seen before. There were no handles on the boxes just a latch with a lock, probably with a key that neither of these two fellows owned. What could be in the boxes and what was this separate road that didn't go anywhere but out? Again, more questions. When would they find some answers? Likely, not tonight anyway.

Meeyha stayed behind as Raeban peeked around the secret door into the pool area. There was no one in the pool or the pool area but how could he be sure that on one was looking from one of the windows above? He pulled his head back and conferred with Meeyha. "We should stay down here a little longer. It's still too light out and I'm afraid some one will see us from above if we leave now."

"Alright, but do we stand here waiting all night?" asked Meeyha with weariness in her voice.

"No, I have an idea," quipped Raeban. "Why don't we spend the night in the conveyance? Let's go down and have a look."

"Are you out of your mind?" exclaimed Meeyha. "What if someone comes down and finds us?"

"We'll get down in the back and hide. It's so big, there must be someplace to hide so we won't be seen. The bigger problem is if someone does come to use the conveyance and we're inside, then we go with them. And if that did happen, I can't even image what would become of us or where we would end up. So the question is: Should we go inside the conveyance at all?"

The question remained unanswered, for as they stood thinking about what to do, they heard voices coming towards them down the stairs. Quickly and quietly they scurried around the back of the conveyance to hide. Feeling their hearts pounding inside their chests, they were sure that someone would hear the pounding and find them. They held their breath. They were afraid beyond belief. Fear of what, they weren't sure, but the overwhelming fear held them rooted to their position as they heard the newcomers coming closer. They could hear the change in volume as they came closer.

"We'd better hurry up and get those other boxes from the Calming Quarters before they lock the back doors" one of the new comers said to the other.

"I don't know what the hurry is," piped in the other, "we could just as easily pick the boxes up in the morning before we leave."

"The Masters had requested them picked up tonight because they need to be delivered as soon as it is light in the morning. And since the doors aren't unlocked before sunrise, we'd be late leaving and, we'd be late delivering the boxes. Apparently, there are a few clients waiting for the supplies . . . . I just wish I knew what's so precious about those supplies and what could be in them, coming from a place like the Calming Quarters" continued the first voice.

"Can't say that I know either, so let's get going and get it done, then we can go in and get something to eat. I haven't eaten all day, all this driving back and forth is killing me" complained the second voice.

Their voices began to fade as they continued talking as they were crossing the courtyard. Meeyha and Raeban cautiously peered around the conveyance to watch where they were going and were surprised at what they saw. There in front of the stand of trees, across the other side of the courtyard the two men melted down into the ground. At least that's what it looked like to Meeyha and Raeban. They mustered their courage and silently ran to where they had last seen the two men.

The gaping hole closed just as Meeyha and Raeban got there. Now out in the open courtyard, they frantically looked up and all around, checking to see how many windows there were that could give away their presence to an onlooker. To their astonishment, there were no windows or doors of any kind. Nothing in that courtyard beyond the trees, a road to nowhere, large slabs of concrete all around one side and now a hole at their feet leading to the Calming Quarters.

This was the type of luck that Meeyha and Raeban were hoping for, an easy entrance into the Calming Quarters so that they could reach Tabina and Banner. But how to open this hole now. It probably worked on a sensor just like the secret door near the pool. So many secrets—and for what? And what was in those boxes the two men were picking up? The fear had completely left them now. Things were becoming very exciting. They could go get Tabina and Banner and get them out of the Calming Quarters and go—where? They had to rethink things again. If only they knew where that conveyance was going in the morning. Just then they had the same thought.

"Why not go with them in the morning." Raeban calmly remarked.

"I was thinking the same thing," Meeyha added excitedly. "That way we can see if escape is possible when we get Tabina and Banner out of the Calming Quarters."

"We can't keep standing here, let's hide and see if we can find out how this thing opens up." Whispered Raeban as he pulled Meeyha with him to hide behind the closest trees. They waited for what they felt was an eternity for the men to return. Then, without warning, the courtyard floor opened and up popped the two men. Still there was no indication how the opening was controlled. But there were the two men with two more shiny boxes in their arms. Meeyha and Raeban watched as the men proceeded to the conveyance and carefully placed the shiny boxes in the back seat of the conveyance. Then the driver gave a quick look around before heading up, saw that the hole was still open, ran back to the edge of the courtyard, just in front of the opening. He gingerly pushed his toe into a small opening in the concrete, and the opening closed. There must be another control inside the hole because when they had entered the hole no one had touched the control. Meeyha and Raeban glanced at each other and smiled a knowing smile. They were going to get Tabina and Banner out. Maybe they should try tonight.

But as it became darker by the second, they decided to leave that part of their plan for later. Tonight they were going to have to prepare to be on that conveyance when it left at sunrise. They walked across the courtyard, once the men had gone back up to the pool area, and checked the conveyance to see if they could find a good hiding place inside for them in the morning. The front had a strange wheel going into the floor and a metal shaft sticking out of the floor beside it. They weren't sure what either were for, but presumed it was a means of moving and directing the conveyance. It would be great if they could find out how to use it but for now they would have to be satisfied if they could find a way to hide in it. There seemed to be a good size compartment in the back of the conveyance so they looked around for a door to open it. They found a latch, they pulled back and upwards on the latch and a square lid lifted away from the compartment. There was their escape hatch! Something made them look again: then realized that if they closed the lid while they were in the compartment they may not be able to open it again from the inside. They would have to think about that before morning. Right now though, it was important to get back up to the pool area and into their room without being seen by too many people. Preferably by no one, if possible. It was already quite dark so they decided it was time they went through. They couldn't stay out there all night, so they held their breath and opened the secret door and stepped out. There were people in the pool and milling around the edges.

That was not what they had expected. There was never anyone around the pool. Now they were trapped. The secret door closed behind them unnoticed, but they couldn't stay behind the planters. Meeyha glanced down at her feet as she edged closer to the building. On the ground, under her feet, was a tunic top, very similar to hers. She stooped down to pick it up. Then very carefully, she took hers off and pulled the new one on. She placed her torn and soiled tunic into the planter, making note to remove it in the morning before anyone was able to find it. Now Raeban was the only one that had a torn and soiled tunic.

Meeyha's heart almost jumped out of her chest, as someone spotted the disturbance they were making behind the planters, and called to her to see if everything was alright. Meeyha stepped out and met Viki's questioning expression. A measure of relief, at seeing a friendly face, gave her the courage to make the first remark that came into her head.

"Viki, I can't believe these trees, they are just wonderful! Raeban and I were admiring them when Raeban feel into one and got all dirty and ripped his tunic. When people came in, we were so embarrassed we didn't want to come out" lied Meeyha in a subdued voice. Raeban just stood there with his mouth open, clearly thinking that Meeyha was the smartest, most beautiful woman in the world.

Viki laughed and led them out of the planters and brought them over to a table laden with such wonderful looking things, that neither Meeyha or Raeban had ever seen before. Apparently it was food, because everyone was eating from the table. But Meeyha and Raeban just gawked at the food, their tummies now really growling. Viki saw their hesitation and gestured to them to try some fresh fruit . . . There were figs, and dates, prickly pears and grapes, none of which they had even heard of, let alone eaten. But they ate and then thanked Viki and hastily left for their room.

Once they got up to their room they didn't know whether to laugh or cry. At this point their poor tummies began to protest wildly. Their tummies had made it very clear that they had never had fresh fruit before and now they were going to pay. They spent sometime in the washroom, which helped them feel better, then they dropped exhausted into bed and immediately feel asleep. Meeyha awoke with a start, then remembered where she was, and shook Raeban awake. She glanced at the bedside table to where the numbers had just changed to read 5:00. That meant that it would be sunrise in about 40 minutes, there was no time to lose. They would have to get to the conveyance before the two men, or else they would lose the opportunity to be on that conveyance when it left. She shook Raeban again. Why wasn't he waking up? Raeban moaned and turned over.

"Wake up!!" shouted Meeyha as loud as she dared. "We have to get going!"

Finally Raeban's eyes opened a slit then shot wide. "Meeyha, why didn't you wake me up sooner, it looks like its starting to get light."

"I tried, sleepy head" she teased, "but you were right out."

"Ready, let's get going or we'll miss our conveyance," Raeban replied as nonchalantly as he could.

"Raeban we haven't solved the lid locking dilemma. What are we going to do? We don't want to get stuck in there and get caught." Cautioned Meeyha.

"We'll think of something, now let's go before the men get there before we do." Replied Raeban pulling on his cloths and shoes.

They hurried down to the reception area and then nonchalantly walked past the attendant to the pool area. He didn't seem to take any notice so they proceeded to the pool area and immediately went to the secret door. It opened as expected and they quickly and quietly fled down the steps. Before they entered the area where the conveyance was waiting, they stopped to listen for any indication that the men were already there. They heard nothing, so they slowly peeked around the door. Good, they had made it, there was no one in sight. Just as they had eased themselves into the rear compartment they heard the men lumbering down the steps. They weren't even trying to be quiet, so they must be pretty certain that no one was around to see the goings on. Meeyha had tied her hair back with a sturdy scarf just before they had left the room. Then she decided, as they had eased themselves into the compartment, to pull the lid down onto the scarf so that it couldn't lock completely. They hoped it would work or they would probably die in the back of that conveyance or they'd be found and likely the same fate would ensue.

As the men checked to see that the boxes were in the back seat where they had left them the night before, the driver noticed that the tires seemed a little low in the back of the conveyance. He mentioned it to the other who suggested they just head out and check the air pressure at the next stop. To Meeyha and Raeban, who couldn't hear very well what was being said outside, felt confident that they were safely hidden and would soon be off.

Finally, it seemed everything was ready. The driver held out his hand to the other. The other looked at the driver and said, "What do you want, let's get going."

"Give me the delivery instructions, we have to go through the check list before we set out" answered the driver.

"I don't have the delivery instructions, you have them. I gave them to you at the pool last night so that you could go over them before we got down here this morning" replied the other.

With an annoying look, the driver retorted, "That's just great, where do we get another copy this early in the day. We can't leave without them."

"Alright let's just think a minute." Said the other very calmly. "You don't have them and neither do I. I thought I gave them to you but you don't remember getting them. Well we had better go have a look for them. Let's go; you go look in your room anyway and I'll go look in mine and we'll meet back at the pool."

"Fine, but I'm sure they're not in my room," persisted the driver as he followed the other back up to the pool area.

Meeyha and Raeban waited a few seconds, heard nothing so they slowly opened the lid to the compartment. As the two men were arguing outside they had had time to think about what they were doing. They both started having second thoughts, but they each kept their thoughts to themselves. Finally, once the two were gone, Raeban spoke up.

"Meeyha," whispered Raeban, "let's get out of here, this was probably a very bad idea anyway. There's no way we'd be able to get out of the compartment to look around and if we did: what would we do."

"You're right Raeban, as usual," agreed Meeyha. "We certainly didn't plan this out very well." Quietly, and cautiously they climbed out of the compartment and crouched behind the conveyance.

"What should we do now?" asked Meeyha.

"Guess this would be a good time to look into the hole in the road, and find out where it leads. Let's hurry before the two come back and see us" Raeban whispered as he pulled Meeyha towards where they had seen the opening in the courtyard the day before.

Raeban poked his toe into the opening in the curb and the ground beside them opened to reveal a small landing just a small steep step down. Beyond was another step and then a long, tunnel that continued beyond where the emerging daylight revealed. As they stepped off of the landing it slowly dropped down the height of an average man, then the opening quietly closed above them and they were in complete darkness.

"Wow!" exclaimed Raeban, "I didn't expect that. Those fellows had to go back to close the hole, it didn't just close on its own. We'd better make sure we know how to open it when we come back. Help me look around or feel around for something that'll release the door."

They systematically ran their hands all along each wall in order not to miss a spot. There was only a soft glow in the tunnel, now that they had been down there for a few minutes, but their vision was still was greatly impaired. Their search was unsuccessful. Panic was beginning to take hold again when Meeyha whispered excitedly, "Raeban, there's probably a foot lever the same as the one outside."

"Good idea, you pass your toe along that wall and I'll do this one" Raeban replied with new hope in his voice. And sure enough, just two feet away from the second step down, there was the toe control. They hurriedly looked around to get their bearings then turned their attention back to the toe control and sent the cobblestone square to close the gapping hole above them. The tunnel was lower than expected, just high enough for Meeyha to walk up right. Raeban had to bend a little so as not to scrap his head as he walked. It wasn't wide enough for them to walk abreast so they made their way forward with Raeban leading. Meeyha grabbed Raeban's tunic and held on as he cautiously shuffled forward. Since he couldn't see well enough to stay in the middle of the tunnel Raeban at times bumped into one side of the wall or the other, but all of a sudden he fell forward as he stubbed his toe on another step. It seemed that they had walked for hours, but they couldn't be sure how long it had been. Then about fifty feet ahead they could see a faint light. They hastened to an opening just big enough to allow one person to squeeze through. Meeyha marveled that the two men yesterday had gotten through it.

Raeban stopped just before the opening and turned to Meeyha. "I'll go through first and find out where we are then I'll come back for you."

"Be careful,' cautioned Meeyha as she watched Raeban disappear into the early morning light beyond.

She poked her head out of the opening and saw what appeared to be a memorial. There in front of her was a large concrete monument of three people; a female, a male and a small child in between the two adults. As Meeyha looked around, a little bird just like the one Meeyha had rescued the day before, landed on top of the child's head. She watched the little bird with interest. There weren't very many birds in the complex, but Meeyha was sure she had never seen this kind before. It appeared to be bigger, in the morning light, than it had the day before. Then her attention went back to the monuments. They were facing away from the opening in front of where she stood. It's massive size blocked some of the scene and the Calming Quarters before her. The base of the monument was about four feet wide and eight feet long and the height was almost six feet. As she looked closer at the back of the monument, Meeyha noticed that there was a latch in the centre of the monument. The base appeared to be made of either granite or another type of stone, thus making the latch an unusual addition to the base. She stepped out of the tunnel and drew up for a closer look at the base. The latch was to fasten a one foot square opening in the top of the base. The ground around the monument was a large oval and was covered with the same cobblestones, except for a small section at her feet, that had been in the courtyard beyond the tunnel. Again, Meeyha took a closer look at the area at her feet and found that it was smoother than the cobblestones. What was this, a burial place, a gravesite, thought Meeyha; she shivered. She wasn't cold, but somehow this place made her uneasy. The tunnel itself hadn't been cold and scary but out here she felt very anxious. She waited impatiently for Raeban and breathed a sigh of relief when she finally saw him.

"Meeyha, this is it, that's the back of the Calming Quarters," whispered Raeban. "There's no one out here but it sounds like things are starting to liven up inside."

"What should we do?" asked Meeyha. "Do you think that door is still locked? Do you think maybe we could go in and look around if its unlocked?"

"I don't know: I don't know: and no! What makes you think we can just go in and look around?" responded Raeban to all her questions but with not too much conviction. As they stood wondering what their next move should be they saw a man coming towards the monument. They hastily squeezed back into the tunnel and waited. The man was carrying two small glass containers in his hands and inside was a gray powdery looking substance. Meeyha and Raeban watched in astonishment at what he did next. He came around the back of the monuments and lifted the latch and pulled up the opening. Then he poured the contents of the containers into the base and replaced the lid and latched it. He mumbled something unintelligible and walked back to the small building extending from the side of the Calming Quarters. Meeyha and Raeban waited a few seconds, allowing the man to walk a safe distance away, then squeezed back out of the tunnel. As they crept around the monument, in the direction that the man had taken, they saw what looked like a small square stone building. There were no windows visible from this side but the connecting bridge, from the main building, was made totally of glass. All along the glass bridge there were hundreds of potted plants of all sizes and colours, hanging from the roof of the glass bridge and sitting on the floor down the entire length of the bridge.

Meeyha and Raeban, glanced at each other, held their breath, then quietly and, as quickly as their legs would take them, headed for the back door, hiding behind the shrubs and plants as they went. Somehow they knew it would have to be now or never to make their visit inside the Calming Quarters.

Chapter 10

Another day, thought Tabina, and no way of getting out of here. She looked over at where Banner was sleeping inhaling evenly and softly in a seemingly restful sleep. Only Tabina was sure it was not so restful. She remembered all too well how disoriented she had felt every time she awoke from being drugged with those yellow pills. Banner would probably take quite a long time, since he had been on them longer than she, coming out of the effects of those pills. She just hoped that once the escape opportunity came she could get Banner roused enough to be able to walk out on his own. If she couldn't then the chance of escaping would be next to nonexistent. But she had to keep her hopes up.

If her calculations were correct the Masters would be back tomorrow so tonight she couldn't go wandering around the floors. But she had managed to visit the two lower floors the night before and all the healing assistants were sleeping as expected. That seemed a little strange since surly one person should be awake somewhere in this type of building. But it worked well for her, so she didn't worry about it. At the end of the second floor there was a large room with two tables at the centre. Along the outside of each bed were a series of trays, all covered with towels. In between both beds were what looked like shiny, silver boxes, piled three boxes deep. The walls in the room were completely covered with cupboards with glass showing supplies used during the surgeries that obviously took place in here. There was a deep shiny, silver sink against the wall with two long necked taps. There were two huge handles on either side of the each tap. Tabina stared at the scene wondering what went on in here, and if Banner was brought down here when they took him from the room.

On one wall, there was a large space, between the cupboards, with two large drawings of the human body. Both male and female organs were clearly depicted on the drawings. Tabina came closer to the drawings and wondered why only these drawings were so prominently illustrated. Did these pictures have anything to do with why they were here. Then just as she drew closer to the drawings she noticed a list of names along the side of each drawing. She looked down the list along the female drawing and noticed many unfamiliar names. Then next to the last name was her name. She knew it was her name. Everyone in the compound had only one name. And everyone's name was unique. The Masters had taken great care in that regard. She remembered being told that it was to ensure that the paired children were not genetically related. Her heart skipped a beat as she hurried over to the male drawing, and sure enough, there was Banner's name along with a dozen other names.

Were all these people here now? And what did this all mean? Tabina couldn't begin to understand the implications. But she knew she was going to do a little more exploring before the healing assistants woke up. She stealthily approached the desk in the middle of the unit and looked around for anything that would hold the names of the patients. Then she saw the computer screen with the name 'Meeyha' on it. And for the second time that night, her heart seemed like it would hammer its way out of her chest. She furtively read on. Again, it was difficult to decipher the meaning of the words because of her lack of knowledge of medical terminology, but she understood enough to know that 'Meeyha' was either here in the building or she was expected. The date that appeared on the screen was from two days earlier. This was just too much. Tabina knew she had to hurry and see if she could check each bed before the healing assistants woke up. Fear and panic gave her renewed impetus to achieve what she had set out to do. All was quiet and each patient lay sleeping as expected. But as Tabina made her way from one room to the next and from patient to patient she was sure Meeyha wasn't here yet. At least not on this floor. That meant that she would have to go check the rooms on the floors above and below. But could she do it tonight? It was very unlikely that she could. Time was running out. If she was to check properly, she would have to wait for tomorrow night. As she hurried back up to the third floor, she heard the healing assistant that was left to monitor the floor, give a big yawn and stretch. She knew her exploring time was over.

The healing assistant in charge on her floor was also awake and was beginning to rouse. The other healing assistants down the hall would probably be rousing soon too, which wouldn't give Tabina much time to check many more rooms. She hesitated for a few moments but Tabina couldn't stay in the hall any longer. She had to get back into her room before she was noticed. But here was another problem now. Should she and Banner still try to leave here or should they stay and wait until Meeyha showed up. Not that Tabina would know when that was but, if Meeyha's name was listed on the computer screen downstairs then maybe she would be brought there. As she was pondering the news, she made a quick decision to check the exit door two floors down. She had to know if the door to the back of the building was unlocked or if it would mean the end to all her plans. She knew she could get down there and back in less than twenty minutes if she hurried. But could she hurry and be quiet and careful not to be seen all at the same time? She must try, she felt that this knowledge was going to be very important soon. And there may not be another opportunity if she waited any longer. Just as she got to the bottom of the second set of stairs, which faced the back door, the side wall opened up and out came an assistant in training, pushing a stretcher. She quickly backed up around the corner and watched as he turned the corner heading in the direction of the lower floor. As he turned, the sheet, covering a human form, started to shift and revealed a woman's hand and lower arm. Tabina quickly inhaled and clasped her hand to her mouth. Her body froze but in a split second she turned and hurried back up to her room.

Chapter 11

Meeyha and Raeban reached the back door, out of breath and filled with fear. They paused just enough for Raeban to try the door. It came open and they slid the short distance across the floor to a couple of large planters with shrubs growing inside. The shrubs were a very welcome sight for, just as they managed to get behind them, the side wall, across from the planters, opened up to reveal a stretcher holding a human form covered by a white sheet. Pushing the stretcher was an assistant in training. As he turned the corner, heading to the lower floor, the sheet shifted and exposed a woman's hand and arm.

Meeyha's eyes opened wide then her vision started to fade and she collapsed into the shrub. Raeban caught her before she and the shrub could tumble onto the hard stone floor. "Meeyha! Meeyha!" urgently whispered Raeban into Meeyha's ear. Meeyha slowly came to and started to feel ill again. This time she composed herself and turned to whisper to Raeban with tears running down her face. "That was Tabina. Was that Tabina? Raeban, that was Tabina!"

"No, Meeyha, no it wasn't Tabina" Raeban placated.

"That was Tabina, Raeban, that was her hand and her arm I saw" Meeyha persisted.

"No, Meeyha, that wasn't Tabina. The sheet shifted and I saw her hair. It was black, not yellow. It's not Tabina! Now lets hurry and see where he was going with her" Responded Raeban and pulled her out of their hiding place.

They followed quickly in the direction they had seen the stretcher go. The assistant in training and the stretcher were near the end of the long hall. As they watched he pushed the stretcher through the glass door and into the long bridge that they had seen from the outside. They continued to watch as he pushed the stretcher through the doors of the small building with the words 'The Potting Shed' written above the open doors.

Raeban gently pulled Meeyha across to a small cabinet filled with pictures of Calming Masters and plaques presented in their honour for services rendered. They hid there for a few minutes until they saw the assistant in training emerge from the small building. They panicked momentarily, but not having anywhere else to hide, they stayed where they were and waited for the young man to approach them.

"Morning" he said brightly. "Are you the two new jobbers?" He continued before they could reply, "They need some help on the second floor. Just go up to the operating rooms and someone there will give you your assignments. And don't worry about your tunics," he added as he noticed Meeyha looking at her tunic then back at his white, pristine tunic, "there's a large linen storage room just past the operating rooms where you can find the white tunics to put over your own." He then turned to walk away.

"Oh, by the way. I didn't get your names" he queried just as they were about to leave down the hall.

"Her name is Meeyh . . . er Mei and my name is Rai," stumbled Raeban. He just hopped that it would appear as nervousness and not that he had just lied about their names.

"Nice to meet you both." And then he walked briskly down the hall and past the stairs and the planters with the shrubs.

Their fear now eased a little. The assistant in training hadn't been alarmed at their presence and they were safe for a time. But now another problem posed itself. What would they do when they got upstairs and didn't have a clue at what was expected? How were they going to get out of the one? But, since they had no choice, they turned around, went down the hall and up the stairs to the two operating rooms.

When they reached the operating rooms there was a healing assistant, and a Calming Master standing beside a patient on a stretcher. They had obviously finished their procedure for the patient as wide awake with a shocked look on his face. There wasn't any evidence of a surgical procedure but the patient's gown was askew across his abdomen. And there on the counter beside the operating table was the mysterious shiny silver box. The lid was open, with small vials neatly stored in three rows down and three rows across. The walls and the lid of the box were quite thick, probably to protect the vials within. One vial in the box was being replaced by the one in the healing assistants' hand.

During all this the patient hadn't moved or changed the expression on his face. It was a mixture of horror or disbelief or probably both. He didn't seem to be in pain but the surgical sheet was askew and dangling across his middle. Just as Raeban turned to glance at the patient the healing assistant remembered the patient's condition and adjusted the sheet to cover him properly.

Meeyha averted her face. They were both outside the operating room door, so their presence had not been noticed by the group in the operating room. She turned to Raeban, and whispered that she was going to be sick again. He put his arm around her and pulled her beyond the closed door. As he moved backward with Meeyha, another healing assistant came in; she noticed the two waiting outside the operating room door and pointed to Raeban and said: "You: go inside and clean up the mess in there. The healing assistants inside will give you instructions." Then to herself as she turned to face Meeyha "I don't know why they keep sending new jobbers every few days. We have to keep telling them what to do each time." Then to Meeyha, "You: go into the operating room next door. There's a small delivery to be made to the 'The Potting Shed' as soon as possible." With that she turned around and left.

Meeyha was relieved to see her leave but wasn't too sure what she was going to be delivering to 'The Potting Shed'. She glanced at Raeban and motioned good-bye with her hand and stepped out into the hall. Raeban held his breath and went into the operating room.

The healing assistants and the Master in charge all turned to look as he opened the door and walked in. The patient too looked at him as he came in with a strange kind of hope in his expression. But as Raeban just proceeded to clean up the strewn implements and put the disorder to rights, the patient looked away all hope gone from his expression. Raeban had noticed the look but couldn't possibly imagine what the patient had expected from him. The Master removed his soiled tunic, washed his hands and left without a word. The healing assistants hurriedly redressed the waiting patient then wheeled him back to his room. Raeban was alone in the strange operating room not really knowing if what he was accomplishing was what was expected. His eyes then fell on another one of those shiny, silver boxes, but to his dismay, the lid was down and the box had been locked with the same strange locks he had seen on the boxes earlier in the morning. He wandered if the same thing was in those other boxes and where were all these boxes going? Since no answers were emerging he continued with his task until he couldn't think of anything else to do. He thought about Meeyha and her task. He hoped he wasn't too late to accompany her with her delivery to the Potting Shed. He looked into the next operating room but found it deserted. He wondered if he could catch up with her on her way to the Potting Shed and left the operating room in quiet run.

When Meeyha had entered into the second operating room, she was hoping that what she thought she was delivering was not true. But her hopes were dashed when she saw a small form lying on the stretcher covered with a white sheet. Again she began to feel sick, but there was no Raeban to help her through this time. She gritted her teeth, then pulled the stretcher towards her and backed out of the operating room. But as she got out into the hall she had no way of knowing how to get down to the lower level. When she and Raeban had hurried into the building earlier she had seen the wall open up, and the floor just settling into place. An assistant in training was pushing a similar stretcher but she didn't know where or how to operate the opening wall and floor. She deliberately slowed her stride in the hopes that Raeban would turn up to help her out. And this time she was lucky because there he came looking quite funny doing his quiet run.

"Raeban, do you know how to operate the moving wall and floor," Meeyha quietly asked him.

"Meeyha," Raeban responded as quietly in her ear. "I heard the healing assistants call the moving floor, an elevator. Let's not give ourselves away by not knowing these things. And no,

I don't know how it works but let's look, maybe they work like the other secret doors around here."

"I got it Raeban, I just needed a little encouragement." Answered Meeyha. "But do you know what's under the sheet? It's a child. I didn't check to see who it was. I just can't bear to find out."

"You're right not to look, if it was one of the children we taught it would be heartbreaking and we have a lot to think about right now. But in the end maybe what we are doing now may help some other child or person" Wisely answered Raeban, with a sad compassionate look on his face.

The door to the elevator opened and they wheeled the stretcher inside. The door closed and they were stuck with an unmoving elevator. They looked at each other, they looked at the door, they looked all around but there was nothing to tell them how to get moving.

Finally Meeyha, discouraged, asked, "How do we get to the lower level?" Just then a voice replied from nowhere. "Going to lower level."

Meeyha and Raeban were both shocked and elated. They had anticipated spending the rest of the day in the elevator with a deceased child for company. Things were certainly different from their quiet life back in Complex A.

They didn't encounter anyone on their way to the 'The Potting Shed', but once they entered they were met by the same man that Meeyha had seen at the monument earlier that morning. She dared not think about what kept nudging at her brain. But now things were beginning to come together. Raeban beside her, was suddenly very quiet and thoughtful himself.

"So, we have another candidate for laser surgery." Distastefully cackled the man. "You know they make good nourishment for shrubs and plants. Just look at how beautiful all the shrubs and plants are around here."

Meeyha and Raeban were shocked and sickened at this terrible human being standing before them. They couldn't open their mouths, let alone say anything to him. This was beyond anything they had ever encountered. They must be dreaming all this, it just couldn't be happening. To their relief the familiar chime sounded for all to participate in the daily Bend and Stretch routines. They took this opportunity to turn and run from this most vile of places. As they were running they heard the creature behind them shouting after them. "If you wait you can watch and see how its done then help me dispose of the remains: I'll show yooouuu."

Meeyha and Raeban ran down the bridge and back into the Calming Quarters. There had never been a place so misnamed in their memories. And Tabina and Banner were somewhere in this place! They couldn't endure the thought and they would do everything in their power to get them out as soon as possible:

tonight, today, now!! But reason soon prevailed and they tried to remain calm as they thought.

Luck was on their side again. All the healing assistants were preparing incapacitated patients to be brought out for the routines. No one was paying any attention to them. They nonchalantly looked around for sight of either Tabina or Banner and were even bold enough to look into some of the rooms that they passed. To their dismay, one of the healing assistants spotted them and came up to them.

"Look, I know you two are finished with your work, but would you do us a big favour and help with a few of these patients? If you do, we'll make sure you get something to eat when we get back." The healing assistant asked kindly. After what Meeyha and Raeban had just been through they wanted nothing but to leave this place and never come back. But each time the thought of Tabina and Banner came back into heads and they relented. "Sure," as cheerfully as he could, Raeban answered for them both.

"Good, then you can go up to the top floor and help out the healing assistants in training with the patients up there. They are a little more out of it than these down here. Oh, and thank you, that's a big help." The healing assistant then moved on to another patient leaving them to go where they would. But again, this was another opportunity they couldn't miss. They ran up the stairs to the top floor and looked around. There were patients in the halls in wheelchairs and some on stretchers, with both healing assistants, and healing assistants in training, bustling about getting everyone ready to go out. Then, as Meeyha and Raeban were looking for both someone to assist, and Tabina and Banner at the same time, they heard someone shouting. At first they just ignored the calls but then realization kicked in.

"Mei, Rai, over here, I could use your help here" continued shouting the healing assistant in training that they had met earlier. They hurried over to him and their hearts leapt for joy. There was Tabina in a wheelchair with her head hanging down her chest, long yellow hair spilling all around her.

"There, see if you can get this one's hair up and away from her face will you?" Requested the young man. "I don't do well with women's hair."

"My pleasure!" chimed Meeyha. She was absolutely ecstatic, they had been planning and scheming and hoping that they would find Tabina and Banner and here was Tabina just handed to her. But where was Banner? She casually looked around to the stretcher, just inside the door where Tabina had been wheeled from, and there he was. She turned her attention to Tabina's hair hoping against hope that she could talk to her. But her hopes were dashed when she started to pull Tabina's hair back and Tabina just let her head be pulled in whatever direction. Her eyes weren't closed but they seemed to be glazed over, as if she had been drugged, which, given what Meeyha and Raeban had seen, was probably the case. That was fine. Somehow, this was going to work for them. She'd make sure of it: somehow.

Raeban had spotted Banner too and made his way to the stretcher and commenced righting sheets and fluffing the pillow, appearing to be readying Banner for the outing. He glanced over to where Tabina and Meeyha were and gave Meeyha a smile and a wink. Meeyha gave him a broad smile and a nod in return.

Chapter 12

He was pacing back and forth. Something was not right. He should have heard from someone by now. Computer glitches were never like this, they didn't last this long and certainly didn't disrupt so much. The Master of Masters wasn't used to feeling helpless. He was the one in charge, he should not be the one waiting for answers. If someone didn't enlighten him soon, he was going to the Calming Quarters himself. People didn't just get lost in the Compound, there wasn't anywhere they could go: or could they?

Bianca could sense what was going on in the Masters of Masters mind. She had known him since he became the Master in Charge many years before. Her position as the 'Keeper of the Archives' wasn't one of great power or influence, but she did get to see and hear what went on sometimes, when no one thought she was aware. And since her position was very important to both the Master of Masters and the continued existence of the Compound, Bianca was left pretty much on her own. She had been there so long that she was more of a fixture than an individual entity. Thus she had gleamed a lot of information over time, especially how the compound had evolved from the 'Eden Project' in the year 2020 to its present state. The original plans and aspirations for the 'Eden Project' were part of the

Keeper of the Archives most guarded responsibility. And Bianca took her responsibilities very seriously. She knew every aspect of the Project and even how the original plans and aspirations were now deviating.

She had given up all manner of advancement options over the years, in order to remain here. It was like she was meant to be the Keeper of the Archives forever. Even as a small child, she had distanced herself from any involvement, starting from the initial pairing at the mega-school right up to the completion of her educational requirements. She felt that she had a mission: a very important mission, that she must complete. Thus anything that might interfere with her attaining her objective was shunned. She had been too young to do anything about rejecting the initial pairing, but she never participated in any activity required in the pairings. In time she had been released from the mandatory pairing. That was not to say that she had not been aware of her intended partner.

White had been a very serious boy, very studious and very bright, she had been aware of that from the very beginning when they were paired. Everyone of his teachers had given him glowing recommendations. They all felt that he would became a very significant member of the Compound. After Bianca had been released from the mandatory pairing, she had still followed his progress in the mega-school and even went so far as meeting his new partner. Bianca was happy that the Masters were able to pair he and Coral, since the pairings were always completed by the time the children were four years old. After that the bonds had been created and the chance to find another perfect match was very slight. But Coral had been the better match for him, for they worked very well together and both excelled in their work. He had progressed to a Third-level Master in neurosurgery and he had re-wired almost four generation of infants. No Master of neurosurgery had endured so long, but with Coral he had said he could go on forever.

But once Coral had passed away at a very young age the Master in Charge, at the time, thought that White would no longer be able to continue in his work. But he rebounded and threw himself totally into his labors. It was like his very existence depended on it. And possibly, thought Bianca, it did. She felt so very sorry for him back then that, a few times, she had almost gone to comfort him, but her responsibilities had always prevented her. Now she wandered how things might have been if she had. She shook herself and brought herself back to the present and the plight of the Master of Masters.

Bianca sensed that his mind was in turmoil. Any passing observer could grasp that, but Bianca could feel his inner pain and his mental anguish, much like a mother could sense her child's suffering. Her position as the Keeper of the Archives gave her an ability that no one else possessed. Not even any of the Masters. The Archives included the information of every child ever born in the Compound. From the first day that the Eden Project was launched to the present. Every birth and every death was recorded. The parents of each child was recorded. Each pairing that had ever been formed had been recorded. There was nothing about any of the past and present inhabitants, of the Compound, that Bianca could not tell you about. Where they were born, their parents, where they were sent and who they were paired with and who the parents of the partner were, etc. etc. So if you thought about it, Bianca's position was the most important one in the Compound. For it was Bianca who made the decision who was going to be paired with whom. And only she could follow every stage of their lives and that of their off-spring. There were infants, though, that were sent to the Calming Quarters, then mysteriously died. Sometimes she wished she could find out why. But to question was to put ones' self in danger. So Bianca carried on: her knowledge, her secret.

And in keeping with the initial directives, the information had remained top secret. Only one person was responsible for the information held in the Archives and when that person was replaced, their memory would be erased. It had been done this way for a few hundred years and it would continue as such. But Bianca didn't have any intention of leaving her position any time soon.

The Keeper of Archives divisions were many, the most significant one was to ensure that the children were never paired with blood relatives. For this reason, genetic illnesses were very rare at this time. Tests were performed on the new-borns and any defects were dealt with in order of priority. If it was minor and a surgery or medical procedure was sufficient then it was performed. If the defect was major the decision of the infants' fate was left to the Fourth-Level Masters.

For Bianca, this knowledge was worth keeping secret, because her very existence was at risk. So, for almost forty-five years she had paired toddlers together and she had recorded countless births and deaths. And she would continue to do so until she passed away. There was no need to train anyone before then. All the information that the successor would need was recorded to the most mundane detail, the succession would be seamless.

Again Bianca brought herself to the present. What was she to do about the Master of Masters dilemma? She surmised that most of his anguish was the fact that he had created a life outside the Compound, that much she knew. The Eden Projects' very survival was at stake because of this folly. But since Master Svene's father had not followed the law as it had been set down, how could Master Svene be expected to follow that law himself. Now as Master of Masters, Master Svene's responsibilities lay in the well-being of the people in the Compound. Life outside the Compound would be impossible for those within. Their culture had deviated too drastically from their origins for the two worlds to integrate now. And what Master Svene had done could prove to be the undoing of all that the Eden Project had meant to the founding fathers of so many generations ago.

Bianca had decided, she would confront Master Svene and offer her assistance, such as she could give. She had nothing to lose. She was old. She had no family, but then no one else here did either, so what did it matter. She would not be missed. But if she could help Master Svene deal with the problems at hand, then she would be satisfied that she had done her best to preserve life in the Compound. If the inevitable could not be escaped, then she would be integral in the location of blood relatives. Knowing birth parents would be difficult for all of them, but in time family units could be formed and life could continue in the way that it was intended many millennium ago.

Chapter 13

White knocked on the door a second time. If someone didn't answer this time he would leave. He stepped back and turned away, then the door opened. He quickly turned back to the opened door. His eyes opened wide. He hadn't seen that face for many, many long years. Yet still, he remembered every feature as if it had been etched in his mind. Of course, the face had been a lot younger then. He hoped that she recognized him too. She didn't look impressed though. But then he had changed considerably since mega-school. Maybe she didn't recognize him.

"I'm sorry. I hadn't expected to see someone from my distant past" explained Bianca. "As a matter of fact, I had just been thinking—I mean I had been wondering—That is I had hoped—" Bianca stopped talking. What was this? She was stumbling over her words and she didn't know what she wanted to say!

"Bianca?" questioned White. "It's been decades since I've seen you but I remember your face like it was yesterday." Suddenly, the memories of those anguished years in mega-school caught up with him. "Do you remember me?"

"Yes! Yes, I remember you White. How could I forget. You are very famous. You did tremendous work back in your day." Bianca was feeling young again, like she might have felt forty years ago, meeting him for the first time. Then she continued, hoping he wouldn't see what she was feeling, "What brings you here? The Master of Masters office is back down the hall just at the top of the stairs." Bianca couldn't imagine what could have brought him here today. Especially since she had been thinking about him just a few minutes ago.

"Well, to tell the truth," started White "I was hoping that someone might help me with a little problem I'm having."

"Please, come in and tell me what kind of problem it is." Bianca was totally mystified. After all these years, to have White come knocking on her door, but why TODAY?

"How to begin?" White's eyes became unfocused and distant. "I've gotten to know a young couple that live in this complex and I would like to get in touch with them. Is there anyway that someone here could help me with that?"

"I don't understand. Are they not in the complex? Had the young couple requested a 'leave to travel'?" questioned Bianca.

"Not really," answered White. "They actually have been sent to the Cleansing Quarters in preparation for their new positions.

I've tried to send messages to them, but my computer rejects all my entries."

"Well that doesn't sound right" offered Bianca. "Did you want me to try sending a message for you?"

"Well, what I really want is to go visit them myself, if I could, that is" as White continued he realized that the request was way out of line. The office for 'Leave to Travel' requests was downstairs in this very building. How could he explain that something drew him up the stairs to this door? He couldn't understand it himself.

"You may have just come to the right place. The Master of Masters was himself thinking of traveling to the Cleansing Quarters. It appears that there has been some disruption of computer correspondence into and out of that entire Complex." Bianca almost bit her tongue. What was she telling him all this for? She hadn't seen him in decades and here he was asking about a young couple on the same day that the Master of Masters was in a dilemma over, more than likely: the same young couple. And why did she tell this fellow, such confidential information? Why? Why? Why?

"Good, I'm so glad. Maybe I should go back and talk to him directly then" now it was White's turn to stumble over his words. Did he really think that the Master of Masters would give him any information about Meeyha and Raeban. Had he lost his big, aged mind? He had decided not to request 'Leave to Travel' and here he was blubbering to the first person he saw about computer problems and missing people. His mind was truly lost.

"Look, I'm sorry. This has been a big mistake. Why don't I just go back home and wait for them to return. Sure, that's what I'm going to do. Thank you for all your help. And, ah, good-bye." With this, White turned on his heel and almost ran down the hall and down the stairs.

Bianca, hung her head. Things weren't going very well today. First the Master of Masters in total turmoil. Now someone from her past just happens to come knocking on her door. And she wanting to help. Help with what? Who was she going to help? How was she going to help? Were they all going out of their minds?

'There you go Bianca,' her mind told her, 'there's your opportunity to get together with White. He obviously needs someone to help him. And you WERE thinking about him earlier. So why don't you go run after him and offer to help search for the young couple.' Her mind went blank.

Bianca stood there, with the door open, staring down at her feet. She willed her feet to move, freeing her from making a deliberate decision. Still they didn't move. How long had she been standing there. She couldn't remember: seconds, minutes, hours? There was no telling. Finally her feet started to move tentatively forward, then momentum was taking her at a run down the stairs and out into the street. She stopped, looked up and down the street. No sign of White. Which way would he go? She hadn't even known that he lived in this Complex, let alone in which direction his unit would be. But maybe he hadn't gone back to his unit, maybe he had gone the other way. But which way was that way? She pondered the question for a while, then decided to go towards the direction of the Cleansing Quarters. This was madness anyway. The Cleansing Quarters was a least ten miles away. Was she going to walk there: and since her feet were still moving, she guessed she was.

White had walked briskly for about thirty minutes. He stepped into the green foliage that grew along the road. He wasn't sure what these green plants were, he never really gave them a second thought. He supposed that they were for producing oxygen through the process of photosynthesis, he and all the other children learned that many decades before in the mega-school, but he also thought these plants may be used for human consumption. No reason why he was thinking about this now. He was only trying to gather his thoughts and figure out why, exactly, he was doing this. It was like his body belonged to someone else. He did as it requested and followed where his feet lead. Surly, he was not expected to walk to the Cleansing Quarters. But who was expecting him to do so? He couldn't answer that one.

No, there was no good reason for him to be sitting here in the dirt. No conveyances came along, and even if they did, what was he going to do, ask them to stop and bring him to the

Cleansing Quarters? They would think he was mad. He lay his head down on his bent knees and immediately fell asleep.

There were birds chirping and cheeping all around him. The noise was loud but not unpleasant, he felt happy and safe in the midst of all those birds. Then one of the birds fell to the ground and lay there, eyes wide open and beak slowly opening and closing. It was like the poor thing couldn't catch his breath.

White woke up with a start. He felt a slight pressure pushing on his chest and his heart was pounding, making his breath come in slow gasps. Was he still dreaming or was he having a heart attack. Well, this was a good place for a heart attack: all alone in the middle of no where, with no one in sight. Now that wasn't true; there was someone coming down the street. Maybe he should get up and let them know he was here. But he was so tired, he just couldn't move. They would probably see him when they got a little closer. Then he noticed who it was. What was she doing here? Did she follow him? Well, he could ask her directly once she got closer. Then all went black and he fell backwards into the green plants.

Bianca had run from the edge of the buildings but now thought she'd better slow down. She would never make it if she pushed herself too much. She wasn't getting any younger and running was not something she did everyday. Glancing around as she was walking, she noticed that the green plants, along this side of the road, were really quite tall now. She remembered them from earlier in the year, when she had taken a little walk to help clear her mind. The Master of Masters had sent a young couple a 'fireplace' and the unthinkable had happened. The fireplace had exploded and had almost killed the young woman. Bianca remembered that now because she had sat down in the dirt in the middle of the plants, just like that man was doing now. Only he was lying down with his white hair spilling in every direction.

As she came closer she realized that it was White and that he wasn't moving. She hurried to his side and felt for his pulse. It was there, slow and faint but still there. Thankfully she had replaced her personal communicator with a new one just today, since her previous one had mysteriously died yesterday. No time to send a polite message to the Medical Building, she sent an urgent appeal, directly to the Emergency Rescue Units station, requesting immediate assistance. Moments later, it seemed to Bianca, they were there putting White onto a stretcher and loading him into the E.R.U. She hesitated then decided she would go along with them to the Medical Building.

Chapter 14

What was that noise? Someone was knocking at the door. Who would be so bold as to keep knocking when he didn't want to be disturbed. Finally Master Svene called out and bid them enter. No one came. Master Svene had had enough, he got up and went to the outer door and opened it with more force than necessary. To his astonishment there was no one there. Either his mind was playing tricks on him or he had heard knocking onto another door. In any case there was no one here, so he slowly walked back to his spacious office.

The windows were large and overlooked a good portion of the complex. If he stood very close, he could see down both sides of the units across the complex directly in front of his building. It may not have been the best choice, way back in the early days of the project, removed as it was from close proximity to the mega-school, but now it provided him a good visual of the units' daily goings on in this complex. It wasn't really necessary to keep an eye on them for everyone had a job to do and they did it to the best of their ability and that was that. The system had been working admirably, his forefathers would have been proud of the successes the project had achieved. The brain re-wiring had been the best thing that could have been recommended by the forwarding thinking—founding fathers.

Once the infants had been re-wired there was no longer any concern that they would be rebellious. All those unsavoury traits, that their ancient ancestors constantly struggled to repress, generally unsuccessfully, were non-existent in the inhabitants of the compound. Of course, the founding fathers themselves had been exempted from having the re-wiring performed on their own off-spring. There had to be a chain of command to empower the re-wired children with values and skills, as well as scheduled duties to be performed without question. The system had been working just fine: up until now. But there were occasional hints, now and then, that things were deviating.

And Master Svene was perturbed. He didn't remember when things started getting out of hand. It was probably after he had started to travel back and forth to see his family outside the dome that he began missing the subtle clues that things might be unravelling. The broad minded original, engineers had gone to great lengths to prevent any leak of information about the condition of the rest of the planet outside the dome, for just that reason.

The dome itself had been an accomplishment of the highest calibre. There had been domes built centuries before, confining or covering any number of objects. From sport facilities, to crops, airports terminals, and hotel complexes, to small collections of buildings: the domes had been widely used during the early 20th and 21st centuries. Then, with the formation of, what the original founding fathers called, The Eden Project, the idea of this particular type of dome had been conceived.

And what an enterprising feat that had proved to be. Not only did the founding fathers find the most suitable location, with a perfect climate, but also the most dreaded location where their presence might never be uncovered. It had been a prohibited site all the way back to the 20th century. The story back then was that aliens had landed on the earth and that a complex had been built at this location to house these aliens and study them without any interference from governmental or private enterprises. There had also been experimentation on the early atomic bombs, with detonations in the surrounding area, which had made the site even more dangerous to human life. Thus when the forefathers were searching for an appropriate site, this proved to be the perfect location. They could not have created a more suitable setting for their project.

When the idea of the dome, to cover the entire site, was put forth it was thought to be an impossible endeavour. To cover, successfully an area this vast, and still maintain the illusion of sky with no visible supports, unimaginable. But the determined forefathers underestimated even their own abilities. This dome, to Master Svene's knowledge, had never been duplicated anywhere in the world. Of course, he hadn't visited the entire globe. There would not have been enough time for him to do so, but with all the news and information, that he was able collect while he was with his family, there was never any indication of a similar venture. Maybe one day he would actually plan to locate any similar endeavors. But today he had other things on his mind.

Yes, Master Svene was sure that the problems began when he started to visit his family more often. He thought back to the first time there had been a computer glitch. It was the same day that he had returned from visiting his family after his father had passed away. Having to take over the position of Master of Masters had been a very overwhelming task, under the circumstances. His father had been grooming him for the job for many years, and Master Svene had felt confident that he was ready for the position. But he never expected that his father would not be there to lend support, if needed. His mother too, having been from the outside world, and normally a very strong, independent woman, had became very distressed when his father suddenly passed away. He had been receiving and sending messages, back and forth to his family, almost constantly during those first few days when he had to come back.

As he thought about that now, he realized that he must have been the one contaminating the signals within the dome. The electronic engineers had succeeded, up to this point, in preventing electronic signals from passing back and forth between the compound and the outside. The outside signals had been constantly trying to penetrate the dome, but the shield, conceived by the engineers, had always managed to kept them out. But, once the shield had been compromised, the fissures present in the dome's make-up had permitted the signals to penetrate, resulting in interference with the computers inside the dome. Better find a solution soon or everything could come crashing down around them.

That was it! Master Svene finally realized why he wasn't getting information from the Calming Quarters. The computers had already been infected and the virus was spreading throughout the system. It was about time someone had realized the problem. But again, who else would image what the problem could be. He had been the sole culprit, so it was up to him to offer the solution for the problem: and without incriminating himself.

He immediately got in touch with the computer engineers and offered a solution to the present problem, knowing that they would be perceptive enough to understand but also naïve enough not to put the pieces together. The problem should be fixed in no time and things could go back to normal. There was big load off his mind.

During all this time, as he was reminiscing, Master Svene had been standing at the window, looking out but not absorbing the scene being played below him. He had watched White leave the building walking in long, purposeful strides. Then a little later he watched as Bianca went flying out of the building, paused, looked this way and that, then ran in the same direction that White had gone. Still he stood there at of his window, deep in thought. Finally, when the E.R.U. went speeding past he came to himself and really looked out the window. His line of vision did not go beyond the end of the units to the road, but the E.R.U. had continued beyond that line of vision so something must have happened on the road. Should he go see what had happened or should he just wait for Bianca to come back and question her?

What was he going to do? Keep waiting? Wait for the Calming Quarters to send acknowledgment that the visitors had arrived? Keep waiting to see what was happening with Bianca? Wait until the computers were properly functioning again? Master Svene didn't like to wait. He wanted to know what he needed so that he could plan the next move.

Chapter 15

White opened his eyes and the first person he saw was Bianca. He was pleased but something was puzzling. Then he looked around and found that he wasn't lying in the dirt any longer, but in the 'Medical Building' emergency room. He remembered falling asleep in the midst of the green plants but after that, there was nothing.

"Can anyone tell me what happened?" timidly asked White of anyone who would answer. Besides Bianca, a healing assistant and a Healing Master were in the room.

"Not to worry," informed the Healing Master "you just over exerted yourself and your body shut down for a few minutes to give your heart a rest. That lazy valve, that was repaired when you were born, just needed a little adjustment, now it's as good as new. Just rest for a few hours then you can get back to enjoying your retirement." And with that piece of advice the Healing Master turned and walked away. Bianca gave White a relieved smile and patted him gently on the shoulder. White looked at Bianca and tears started to form in his eyes. No one had shown such concern for him in a very long time and all the pent up emotions, which should not have been possible, surfaced. Bianca noticed his features soften and discreetly lowered her eyes and proceeded to straighten the bed sheets around him.

"I hope you don't mind, but I think I'll leave you for a while" casually commented Bianca, then continued with "I'm just going back to put my office in order, then I'll come back."

White had looked disappointed when she had started to talk then a big smile erupted on his face as she continued. She did not respond to his smile, just waved her hand in farewell, then left. White felt like a new man. His heart had settled into a nice, easy, rhythmic beat. Now, if he could only find a way to get to the Cleansing Quarters and look for Meeyha and Raeban, things would be just great. Then he had a thought. The Healing Master was still in the building. His request for a visit to the Cleansing Quarters would be approved if White requested one from the Healing Master in charge. And that was just what he did.

When Bianca returned she found White up and waiting for her. "How would you like to go to the Cleansing Quarters with me" he immediately asked of her. Bianca looked surprised. This was sudden. Well, if she actually thought about it, it was only an hour ago when she went running after him, to goodness knows where. She said yes, but she must let the Master of Masters know of her absence. Since her position was not one that needed constant attendance, her request would not be denied.

Given that the request for a visit to the Cleansing Quarters had been approved by a Healing Master a conveyance would also be provided and they could leave within the hour. White couldn't have been happier. He marvelled at the changes that had occurred in such a short time. He had lived for years alone and lonely, then over the course of a few months he had found friends, purpose, and a lady who was willing to stay by his side. Life was good again.

The conveyance arrived, promptly and ready to depart, as was promised. To expect otherwise would have been unusual. This was what life had always been like. As children, reasonable requests or behaviours towards the nurturing parents was always rewarded by reasonable responses. It was expected and it was conveyed.

The short journey to the Cleansing Quarters was uneventful. White and Bianca arrived just in time for a beautiful buffet being set up in the pool area. It had been many years since White had been to the Cleansing Quarters and it showed. He was sure he had never seen the pool before. When did that happen, and what exactly was the purpose of it. Water had not been used in such abundance. The only time water was used, was in small fountains, which were set out for the few birds that existed, and for nourishing the plants and shrubs that grew in the complex and in the fields beyond.

The meal was also many times what should have been needed to satisfy the small gathering around the pool. White looked around but did not see anyone familiar, especially the two he had wanted most to see. White didn't tell Bianca everything about Meeyha and Raeban but he did mention that he was hoping to see them at the Cleansing Quarters.

So Meeyha and Raeban weren't at the buffet by the pool. Did that mean the programs that they were participating in had not concluded for the day, or that they had already eaten and gone elsewhere? Maybe they had decided to go for a walk after a long day in a classroom. That may be it. He would just sit and enjoy the pool and Bianca then, and wait for their return.

Night time came but Meeyha and Raeban didn't. White could hear some discourse at the far end of the pool just outside the doorway, but the distance prevented him from hearing exactly what. He strained but to no avail. Bianca had been sitting quietly beside him so he questioned her about the conversation at end of the pool. As Bianca had noticed about herself, many years before and that had proven to be such an aid in amassing much information, was that she had very keen hearing. She was surprised when White asked about the conversation but was pleased to be able to tell him that the conversation was about the matter of two people that had not returned to the Cleansing Quarters.

White's interest was immediately peaked. They might have been talking about Meeyha and Raeban, but how to find out without actually asking? Well, maybe he would try his personal communicator again. See if they would respond now, since they were in close proximity. He told Bianca what he had decided and left her sitting by the pool as he proceeded up to their room. Once there he entered the young couple's communicator address and waited for their response. The computer seemed to be functioning now. But just as it seemed that he would get a response, White heard a crackle and the correspondence was ended before it was actually started. That was very strange. White wanted to try again but thought about where they might be that they would not want to receive a message at this time. Maybe they were indisposed. Maybe they were unable to answer because there was an outside force that prevented them from doing so. So many scenarios to choose from. Which one was the right one? What could he do to help them? If only he knew where they were. The best he could come up with was to leave them a message on the couple's personal computer and wait for them to respond. There was so much going on around here, White felt he should prepare for the worst, one way or another.

As Bianca was sitting waiting for White to return to the pool, she began thinking about this young couple that White was concerned about. She must know who this couple was. What were the names he had mentioned? She thought, but in the end she decided that she may not have been told who they were. Something then brought her back to the young woman who had almost been killed by an exploding fireplace. That was it! That was the young woman White had been talking about. Bianca was sure of it. Now if White would just get back she could see what they could do together to find this missing young couple.

Then to Bianca's dismay, she remembered Master Svene's request when she had gone back to tell him that she was leaving with White to go to the Cleansing Quarters. Better let White know when he got back, there may be a problem brewing there.

Chapter 16

'Well, well, well,' thought Master Svene, 'my Bianca is going to the Cleansing Quarters with White the old revered retired master. How did they get to know each other? She never leaves her precious Archives and he doesn't do anything at all."

Master Svene could not figure out what had brought Bianca and White together. He could have just asked Bianca to explain but that wouldn't have looked too sympathetic. They were both alone so how could he question their desire to pair up now. But so fast, they must have known each other some other time. This was so peculiar. Still, Bianca was the most consistent person in Master Svene's life in the Compound. She was like a second mother, since he visited his real mother so infrequently, as he grew up between the Compound and the outside world. He trusted her almost as much as he trusted himself. But he hoped that his request, for her to check up on the 'visitors' to the Calming Quarters, wasn't too bold. Hopefully, there would be nothing suspicious about the request. No one at the Calming Quarters was going to tell her who the visitors were and they were definitely not going to tell them why they were going there. Now he was beginning to have second thoughts about his request to Bianca. Well, the conveyance should be back by now. It was past dinner hour and he had already been waiting a few hours. He felt it was time that he took a little journey to the Calming Quarters himself, he hadn't been there since that yellow haired girl and her partner had been sent there a several months ago. All this had to be resolved now, once and for all. It was too bad that it had continued so long. That fireplace should have done the trick. Then everything would have been cleaned up and no one the wiser. His hope was that those two weren't still meddling where they didn't belong. He wasn't going to just sit back and let everything, he had achieved, fall apart now.

The last two shipments, from the Calming Quarters, were very well received and so much so that more were demanded. The bright yellow haired children were widely sought after. Master Svene didn't know if he could deliver anymore of the yellow haired female's eggs, let alone anymore yellow haired babies. She had been there, right under his nose, and he wasn't even aware of the appeal that she would have on the outside world. He should have told the Masters at the Calming Quarters to wait and fertilized those eggs with the girl's partner's sperm, instead of taking all the eggs from her. He could have made more money than he could possibly spend. How could he have been so blind? But hopefully, if those other two meddlers could be found before they were able to uncover Tabina and Banner's whereabouts, things could still work out. Master Svene was sure it wasn't too late yet. It couldn't be. It was only a few days since Meeyha was released from the Medical Building, so there could not possibly have been time for them to discover Tabina and Banner at the Calming Quarters. The problem was to find out what those two were doing and where they were hiding? There really weren't any possible hiding places in the Compound. Well, not that were accessible to anyone other than the top level Masters and their associates.

Then he had another very disturbing thought. Was White in league with those two meddlers? If he was, then Master Svene was in deep trouble. White was a third level Master and he knew almost as much about the outside world as Master Svene himself. The system was made up that way: the higher level Masters were trusted unconditionally. They were given access to the Archives that protected the books and information about their existence in the dome and the planet itself. They should not have let White wander around unrestricted after he had retired. Master Svene should have known idle hands created active minds. And that had been the whole point of the infants' brain re-wiring. There should have been no deviation back to the normal, human, emotional states. But because of White's age, it was inevitable that emotions should slowly start seeping back into existence. Now what to do about White, probably the same as what to do about the two meddlers.

Chapter 17

Just as Raeban, with Banner on the stretcher, was about to follow Meeyha, and Tabina in the wheelchair, the healing assistant came back and spoke to Raeban.

"No, no this patient is not to be brought outside today, he's going to be transferred into a wheelchair later" admonished the healing assistant. "Just stay in his room with him if you want to or just go along outside for the practice" continued the healing assistant. She then walked up to another patient in a wheelchair and had totally put Raeban and Banner out of her mind.

Raeban looked for Meeyha and watched her as she wheeled Tabina to the elevator. He was loath to leave Banner but he needed to talk to Meeyha about how they would have to proceed. They could talk as they wheeled Tabina downstairs and hopefully no one would notice what they were talking about.

Meeyha must try to make Tabina understand that they were going to get her and Banner out of the Calming Quarters. But because they didn't know exactly when that would be, there would have to be a way that Tabina and Banner could meet them somewhere once they had an opportunity to try the escape. But where could they hide? Raeban would have to think about that. The elevator arrived at its destination much too soon, there was no way to get all this organized without discussing it with everyone concerned.

Raeban then put his hand on Meeyha's arm and slowed her progress. He whispered in her ear then left to go back upstairs to Banner's room. Meeyha positioned Tabina's wheelchair away from other patients in the hopes of talking to Tabina in private. However a healing assistant came up beside her, leaned over and asked if Meeyha would mind keeping an eye on her patient while she joined the practice.

"I haven't had a chance to practice for a few days now and I really miss it," complained the young healing assistant as she ran past, not waiting for Meeyha's answer.

Meeyha cheerfully acquiesced to the healing assistant's departing back. That was perfect, there was no one else within hearing so she could hopefully make Tabina understand what she and Raeban were going to do. She crouched down in front of Tabina and took her face in her hands and lifted it until it was in line with Meeyha's. As Tabina's eyes focused, they suddenly opened wide Meeyha was delighted. That must certainly mean that Tabina knew who she was, but she went a little further and gingerly asked, "Tabina do you know who I am?" Meeyha waited for Tabina to answer but no reply came.

Instead Tabina's eyes blinked one long blink. Meeyha didn't understand so she ventured another question.

"Tabina is the blinking a way of saying yes or no?" Again Tabina's answer to Meeyha's question was another blink. Again Meeyha wanted to fully confirm that was the case. "If the one long blink means yes, do it again please" Requested Meeyha. Tabina complied with another long blink. Meeyha threw her arms around Tabina and hugged her close to her for a very long time. Then realizing that someone could be watching, she drew herself quickly away. There was indeed hope of saving Tabina and Banner now. If she could give Tabina enough information then they might be able to get away tonight. Of course, if Banner was incapacitated that would be impossible. But she wasn't going to give up just yet. She'd persist as long as she could. The practice would be at least another 20 minutes. Maybe by that time Meeyha would be able to accomplish this most urgent task.

Suddenly Meeyha jumped and suppressed a startled scream. The patient next to her had grabbed her arm and held it in a vice grip. She relaxed a little when she noticed that the patient was looking at her with neither malice nor dislike. The poor dear was expressionless all the while holding onto Meeyha's arm as if it was a life raft. This time Meeyha suppressed a welling of compassion that frightened her more than anything she had experienced so far in her short life. Even the fear of being exposed in the cobblestone courtyard, did not compare with the fear of this new discovery. She gently pried the patient's hand from her arm and spoke to her with a soft, soothing voice.

"Don't be afraid, I'm not going to hurt you, or Tabina here beside you. If you can understand what I'm saying please blink once for me." Meeyha waited patiently for a few seconds, but the expression on the patient's face didn't waiver. Meeyha tried again, this time she crouched down and drew her face directly across from the patient. "Can you hear the words I am saying?' asked Meeyha. No response from the patient. "Blink if you can hear me talking" again Meeyha attempted to elicit a reply. She stayed as she was and gently continued to hold the patients warm face. Slowly the patient's eyes closed and quickly opened. Meeyha was delighted. But she tried another question to make sure that the patient was understanding what was requested. "Is your name Tabina?" Meeyha asked the patient sitting before her. Again the patient slowly blinked, then opened her eyes big and wide. That was the wrong answer. Meeyha wasn't sure if she should persist with the patient. But time was running out, she needed to continue with Tabina. She gently took the patient's hands in hers and told her that she was right there if she needed her. Meeyha left the patient's side and returned to face Tabina.

"Tabina, listen very carefully" Meeyha whispered to her. "Raeban is with Banner right now." At this information Tabina's eyes opened wider than before. Her lips pursed as if she was trying to vocalize some sort of response. "Tabina," Meeyha went on "Banner is not totally awake but he looks alright. But it is very important for you to try to stay awake and help Raeban and I to help you and Banner." Meeyha looked tentatively around then continued, "Is there any way that you can walk?" One long blink from Tabina. "Good" continued Meeyha. She was feeling hopeful again. Meeyha had to think a few seconds. She had to word her requests in such a way that Tabina could answer with the blinks, otherwise she couldn't be sure that the information that was being relayed was understood. She tried again. "Tabina, can you get out of your bed by yourself?" Another long blink. "This is wonderful" cheered Meeyha. "Now this question is going to take a little more effort from you. Are you ready?" Tabina blinked again. "Then tell me, with blinks, at what time can you be out of bed tonight?" Asked Meeyha in anticipation. Tabina thought for a moment, then she began to blink. Once, twice, three times. She continued until she had blinked a total of ten times. Meeyha then asked her, "Are you tired now?" Tabina answered with two quick blinks. A definite no as far Meeyha was concerned. "That's great Tabina. Now, was that at ten o'clock tonight that you can get out of bed?" Meeyha again watched for the blink from the beautiful blue eyes looking back at her. Again the single blink. Meeyha was delighted. She then proceeded to give Tabina instructions as to what to do once she got out of bed.

Meeyha and Raeban would wait for Tabina just outside the back door. There were two large planters just inside the back door, big enough that two people could crouch down behind without being noticed so Tabina definitely wouldn't be noticed. She could wait for them if she got down there before Meeyha and Raeban did. She informed Tabina that the back door was probably going to be locked from the inside, but that neither she nor Raeban knew exactly what time. If, by chance, the door was unlocked and they could get inside, then Meeyha and Raeban would hide behind the planters and wait for Tabina. If Meeyha and Raeban weren't behind the planters then Tabina would have to try to unlock the door for them. So that was set, they would meet at ten o'clock and make their plans to escape.

Tabina gave Meeyha a questioning glance and her mouth moved as if to say "Banner?"

"Are you asking what about Banner?" Meeyha asked of Tabina and she blinked one long blink.

"Tabina you don't have to worry about Banner" reassured Meeyha "Raeban and I will look after him. We'll carry him out if necessary. We won't leave him, or you, behind. If we get caught then we're all going to get caught. No one is going to leave without the other. I promise you Tabina. Raeban and I will do everything we can to get us all out of here. But if you can, please see if there is anyway that Banner can be made aware of what we are going to do. Can I depend on you to tell him, in case that Raeban hasn't been able to inform him?" Meeyha waited for the blink one last time, but as she watched Tabina for that last heartening blink, Tabina rolled her eyes and flopped her head down onto her chest again. Meeyha was devastated. Her resolve almost faltered until she heard the healing assistant behind her, thanking Meeyha for keeping an eye on her patient while she went to the practice. Meeyha now understood what Tabina had done. She was maintaining the rouse that she was totally sedated in order to collect all the information that Meeyha was relaying to her.

Meeyha couldn't believe that the time had gone so fast. The practice must have ended earlier than expected. But no, that wasn't it. Meeyha had been so absorbed by her endeavors with Tabina, that she had lost all track of time. But she was pleased that she was able to convey the information to Tabina without anyone else hearing. She was a little concerned about the patient sitting patiently beside her, but she had not made anymore attempts at grabbing Meeyha again so she relaxed a bit.

Then out of the blue, the healing assistant, that had just thanked Meeyha, took a quick, loud, intake of breath. As Meeyha looked around, her heart beating wildly, she noticed that the healing assistant was trying to shake the patient in the wheelchair awake. The poor dear soul must have passed away while Meeyha was talking to Tabina. She was truly sorry that she had not noticed her passing. But from the look of calm, peacefulness in her face she was now at rest and over all her mysterious ordeals. Meeyha was sure that she must have gone through much, for she was not any older than herself but her facial features had looked strained and weary. Now Meeyha sensed that she was happy again, at last.

The others had started bringing their patients back into the Calming Quarters as well. The unencumbered participants of the practice were also drifting back into the building. It was time for breakfast for the patients and everyone headed to their appointed duties. Meeyha wheeled Tabina upstairs by way of the elevator. But since there were others being transported to the upper levels, there was no further opportunity of discussion with Tabina. Meeyha hoped that she would be able to catch a glance at Tabina's eyes again, just to make sure she was only just faking to be unresponsive. But Meeyha had to content herself with touching Tabina's shoulder as she continued wheeling her back to her room.

Raeban was standing near Banner's wheelchair when Meeyha, Tabina and an unnamed healing assistant came into the room. Banner had the same vacant expression as Tabina. It was hard to determine whether the vacant stare was genuine or contrived for the healing assistant's benefit. But since the healing assistant didn't seem to be concerned, Meeyha and Raeban felt secure in their plot to abduct Tabina and Banner.

The healing assistant looked at Meeyha and Raeban and said, "If you two are hungry I'm sure there are some items left over from the patient's breakfast. Why don't you two go help yourselves while I give these two something to eat. Just come back when you are finished and we'll find something else for you to do."

Meeyha and Raeban looked at each other a little dubiously, then decided it would be best to comply. They could look and listen for anything that could tell them what was planned for Tabina and Banner, so they went off with eyes and ears open.

Chapter 18

When White returned to the pool, Bianca looked a little perturbed. She was looking around as if she was expecting something sinister to happen at any time. Finally she turned around just as White came up to her side then grabbed his arm and pulled him down to her face.

"White, I think I know what's been happening with your two friends" Bianca excitedly blurted out the words. White just looked at her, not quite understanding. She continued, at little more detached "I mean that, while you were gone, I was thinking back over the course of these past few months and some things are beginning to fall into place."

Still White was not comprehending what Bianca was trying to tell him. "What exactly are you speaking about?" White asked warily.

Bianca thought a minute before she proceeded. She looked casually around before speaking again. She didn't want to unduly frighten White, but she must let him see that things weren't quite what they looked like with the Master of Masters. "White there's something you need to understand about the Master of Masters." She started again cautiously, "What we were all taught at the mega-school may not have been how things progressed over the last few decades. It's too much to go into right now, but what started as an imperative objective in the founding father's Cause, seems to have drifted into a malevolent obsession."

At this point White was getting totally frustrated with Bianca. "Please, Bianca could you be a little more explicit with what you are trying to tell me?" Asked White, patiently.

"The Master of Masters is leading a double life and he is totally using our existence here for his own benefit. He has been selling babies for years and just recently he has been harvesting female eggs and male sperm to sell to the outside world." Bianca rushed through what she had to tell him before she could change her mind. It was out now, and it couldn't be taken back. She didn't know what was going to happen now but things were going to change for everyone not just for herself and the two young couples, that White was concerned about, but for the entire program that had been envisioned by the founding fathers.

White hadn't moved a muscle or made a sound for several minutes. He just stared at Bianca with first shock, then disbelief, then anger showing on his face. Bianca squeezed his arm harder to bring him back to her. "White, I can see how this is affecting you, but please let's not rush into anything before we have thought it through."

White considered that for a moment and decided that they needed to go somewhere and get their thoughts together before they acted, as Bianca had suggested. Rushing around demanding answers wasn't going to help at this point. They must find the two couples then see what escape options were available. Deep inside White wasn't sure there were many options, probably only one. And that one option wasn't one that White cared to consider. Once the Masters found anyone that was not upholding the original laws set forth then that someone was taken away and dealt with. But that someone was never seen or heard of again. White didn't want to consider what happened to them other than possibly being re-programmed to comply. Being a neuro-surgeon White knew that there were many ways to re-program the human brain to gain particular results. Only White had not wanted to advance to the level four that gave the Masters that power. He was quite happy to remain free of those decisions whereby he was judge, jury and executioner. Maybe he had been remise, all these years, in his duty as a protector of life. Maybe if he had advanced to level four things would have progressed differently. But was he really so important, in the scheme of things here, that he would have made such a difference in the decisions? Many people had disappeared before him and many more continued now. At this moment, White realized that there was much going on that even he would not have been privy to. But there must be others that were. Who were they; who could help; who could he ask?

As White stood beside Bianca he saw a young lady approach them. Viki came up to the elderly pair and greeted them warmly, "Good evening revered elders. We don't usually see so many people here from Complex A at the same time, but its so nice to see you here and enjoying what we have to offer." As she spoke her face had a much more intense look than the statement would warrant. White looked at her closely then finally answered, "We thank you young miss, but we have not yet encountered any others here from Complex A. Could you please tell us about them so that we may find them and greet them?" And White added his own version of her intense look.

Immediately she understood. Viki had much to tell, but her only offering of information was that she had not seen the pair since the night before. "But Meeyha, that was the lady's name, was so very interested in the Calming Quarters, that she must have gotten her wish to visit the building." This time the look that she gave White, as she delivered the last sentence, was one of worry. White took a deep breath and very quietly asked Viki, "Do you think they are in danger?" With that question Viki simply answered with much relief, "Yes." Then with a sweet smile to both of them she wished them goodnight again and walked away. As she turned from them she hoped that they had understood the implications of Meeyha and Raeban's wish to visit the 'Calming Quarters.' She could do no more than to offer the elderly pair help if they requested it of her.

White and Bianca, by this time, had made up their minds that they would see if she would assist them further, then followed her back inside to the reception desk. She was writing on a piece of paper as they approached her. When they reached the desk, she very stealthily folded the piece of paper and handed it to White. He took it, and walked away, arm in arm with Bianca. They continued walking outside to the front of the building and down the street.

A short distance away from the Cleansing Quarters White brought the piece of paper out and read its contents. He looked at Bianca and told her that Viki had asked them to meet her back at the pool at 2300 hours, she had some information for them. White and Bianca were excited, but their excitement was one of fear and apprehension, not of pleasure, for they had a feeling that what they were about to embark on could be very dangerous.

At last it was 2300 hours, and as White and Bianca quietly walked back down to the pool area, a little groggy from the interruption to their sleep, they saw no one. They sat down in the chairs they had used earlier that evening and patiently waited for Viki. Then, as if out of nowhere, there she was standing in front of a bank of huge planters over beside a short wall on the other side of the pool. She beckoned them to her, and, as she waved her hand above her head, the wall behind her slid quietly open. When they approached, they could just discern a darker large opening behind her, then were surprised as she turned and melted into the darkness. They followed as she beckoned them. Once inside the opening complete darkness enveloped them all. Viki produced a small light and continued down the steps with White and Bianca close behind. At the bottom of the steps, Viki stopped and lead them to a small room where her light illuminated the area where they stood. The room's only furniture was a table and two chairs neatly pulled up to the table: nothing else just three items. If they had been of another era, they might have thought it to be an interrogation room, but such need of a room was completely alien to them.

Immediately that they entered the room, Viki notified them of her concerns, "I'm so glad that you came tonight. I'm very worried about Meeyha and Raeban. As you can see, there is more to the Cleansing Quarters than meets the eye. This continues to a courtyard which houses a conveyance, such as you have probably never seen. Beyond that is a tunnel that connects to the Calming Quarters. I believe that the two of them have taken the tunnel to the Calming Quarters and are still there. As you may know, the Calming Quarters are not open to everyone to enter as they please, and since I have not seen or heard of them since two evenings ago, I feel that they are there and in danger. Could you, or would you, be able to help them?"

White and Bianca had remained silent during all this and now it was Bianca that questioned Viki. "How do we know that you are not the one that put them, and now us, in danger?"

"You are wise to ask, but as I said before the Cleansing Quarters, and the Calming Quarters are not all that they seem. There are a lot of things going on here that would be best that none of us knew about. But we do, and by we, I mean my partner and I, and probably your friends too by now. Although you may know yourselves, that there is more to the Cleansing and Calming Quarters, than you may want to admit."

Bianca persisted again, "If we are to be of any assistance, which I'm not saying we can be, you will have to tell us what is going on and what it has to do with us?" Viki remained calm and told them all she knew as succinctly as she could. There was no time to waste and if there was help to be had it would have to be sooner rather than later. White and Bianca listened then White replied for them both, "Thank you for trusting us with that information. And yes, we will try to help, but we are old and may not be as useful as you think. Tell us what we can do and we'll do our best."

Viki then explained about the tunnel and how it connected the two buildings together and that they could get safely across to the Calming Quarters that way. Valtre, Viki's partner, worked in the Cleansing Quarters and was very familiar with the building; the rooms, all the corridors and where they led; the banks of computers (that linked all the personal communicators and computers to each other); mechanical devices that operated the dome perimeters, as well as the gateways to the outside world. He had been maintaining all the computer and mechanical devices in the complex and thus become aware of what their existence was about inside the dome, and that the world outside was not toxic or had been totally destroyed, as they had been programmed to believe.

Viki told White and Bianca further, that if they could bring Meeyha and Raeban here, then she and Valtre could see about getting the six of them out of the dome. At this last comment White looked at Viki, his disbelief clearly showing on his face. "What do you mean get the six of us out of the dome? Where would we go and how would we get there?"

"I know all this sounds far fetched, but once one leaves the confines of the dome, it is possible to live in the outside world. The only thing needed is someone, a higher level Master, who can enlighten the proper authorities in the outside world, about what has been going on in this Compound over these past few centuries." Viki was becoming a little more passionate now. She had remained calm for so long, now she was letting her passion for life and righteousness come forward, no longer afraid to let it show. "We need you, revered aged Master, to help us do it." At this point Viki was almost pleading. She composed herself and said, "we need to hurry, time is fleeting. The conveyance down here can take us through to the outside world. It's just a few minutes beyond. There we could reach the authorities and inform them of this place and request help for the people here. But we need to be persuasive and credible with some kind of proof that we exist in some kind of captivity. Again, will you help us?"

"Of course we'll help. We are at your command. Right White?" This came from Bianca for she had much to tell the authorities. Her archives could tell the entire story and she was certainly willing to part with them. But they were probably beyond her reach now, but she would try to retrieve them if it was humanly possible. The only way now was for Bianca to recall as much of the contents of the Archives that she could. They could discuss that later.

Chapter 19

Tabina was lucky, Banner was still awake. He had needed help to eat his breakfast but at least he could hold his head up without it flopping down to his chest after every bite as the healing assistant helped him. She watched carefully for the healing assistant approaching with the well-known meds. She was wide awake now, but was careful not to show just how wide awake to the healing assistant. She wanted to intercept Banner's meds before he swallowed them. Finally the healing assistant took the tray, with the remains of Banner's breakfast, and left the room.

"Banner, can you hear me?" whispered Tabina as she watched his every move. "Banner, do something if you can hear me." She tried again as loudly as she dared and watched his head, his hands, his feet. Nothing happened. "Banner, try, please try, to move your fingers or hand if you can."

Then to Tabina's delight, Banner moved his left thumb up and down several times on his lap. He stopped for a few seconds then his entire hand started to twitch. She gave him some encouragement and then requested further. "Banner listen to me. When the healing assistant comes with your meds don't swallow. Just tuck them between your teeth and your cheek and I'll come take them out. Understand? Let me know you understand." Then she watched as he started to lift his head ever so slowly up a short way then down to his chest. "If that was a yes, move your thumb again three times so that I can be sure." She watched as he did so. "Good, now just stay there until they come, and be careful not to swallow the pills when the healing assistant gives you water."

Instead of the healing assistant Tabina noticed that it was Meeyha and Raeban that came quickly and quietly into the room. She looked right into Meeyha's face and gave her small smile, careful not to create too much animation. She whispered, as Meeyha approached her with an answering smile on her own face. "I've told Banner not to swallow the meds when he gets them. So maybe I can keep him awake until tonight."

Meeyha patted her hand and said, "I'm so glad you're awake and talking. I was afraid earlier that you didn't understand what I had told you." Tabina nodded and she resumed her previous expression when the healing assistant came back into the room.

"Oh you two are back? Well let's just see if we can get you to do a few more things before you leave. Here hold the glass while I give the patient his meds, then you can give him a few small drinks until he swallows the pills." With that she popped two little pills into Banner's mouth and walked out of the room. Meeyha took the opportunity to retrieve the pills herself, and gleefully looked at Tabina as she furtively displayed the pills.

Tabina smiled. Meeyha proceeded to give Banner a few sips of water and slipped the two pills into her pocket.

When the healing assistant came back into the room she spoke to Meeyha and Raeban. "It looks like the entire floor is covered with soiled linen, so if you could help the cleaning staff to move all this stuff down to the laundry room that would be a great help."

Meeyha and Raeban were both delighted and apprehensive about their new chore. Delighted that they could get to stay a little longer to be with Tabina and Banner, but apprehensive about exposing themselves further. They gave Tabina and Banner a last word of encouragement and reminded them about their rendezvous later that evening. They collected the soiled linens into the large wheeled hamper and proceeded to the lower level.

The laundry room was in the opposite direction of the Potting Shed. Meeyha shivered as she thought of the real meaning of that Potting Shed. That was how they disposed of those poor people that died. There was no ceremonial service or comforting words or even a short remembrance of the person's life. Once a person passed away they were instantly reduced to a pile of ashes that were then used to nourish the plants and shrubs. Meeyha didn't know why, but she knew that just wasn't right. It didn't feel right. It was like they were really nothing at all, they were of no importance once their life was over. Only if you were a great 'Master' did even one picture remain of your existence in the dome. Meeyha wanted to speak to Raeban but there were people in the laundry room as they approached with the soiled linen, so she kept her mounting melancholic feelings to herself. They deposited the soiled linen where indicated and took the wheeled hamper away to the storage area. Raeban took a good look around and committed the details to memory. You never know when you might need a wheeled hamper when you're trying to escape from a potentially dangerous situation. A final look about and they quickly left the steamy, foul smelling laundry room.

Since no one else approached them with new duties, Meeyha and Raeban were a little nervous just hovering around the Calming Quarters. They wanted to stay close to Tabina and Banner but were afraid that someone would become suspicious of two idle jobbers hovering in the halls. So quietly and quickly they headed to the next level and the back door.

"Just where do you two think you are going?" came a voice behind them just as they reached the top of the steps. They looked around to face the rather unpleasant healing assistant from the operating room earlier in the morning. "You haven't been dismissed yet: there are four huge trolleys with clean linen that need to be distributed. That should keep you two busy until dinner time. When you have all the linen put away, then you can have dinner before you leave. But mind you get all the linen put away, or no one leaves here until it's done." Meeyha and Raeban were feeling slightly relieved that they didn't have to leave just yet, but were concerned that they may not be allowed to leave in time to meet Tabina and Banner.

But they were determined to be ready: even if they had to forgo dinner in order to do so. They promptly nodded to the healing assistant and continued up the stairs. "Not that way," loudly corrected the healing assistant, "the clean linen is on the other side of the laundry room, down this corridor." She pointed towards the corridor that lead to the Potting Shed. Meeyha swallowed noisily and followed Raeban as he headed in the right direction.

"The healing assistant was right about the trolley's being huge." complained Meeyha. "I've never had to move anything this heavy before. It could take me all day just to get one trolley from one place to another."

"Don't worry, we'll do the trolleys together. That way I can bring the trolleys to the floors and you can empty them until I get back to you. Just let's not underestimate the time we have to do it in." Raeban reassured Meeyha as he pushed the huge trolley to the elevator.

Emptying the trolleys did indeed take the better part of the afternoon. In the meantime, they were able to briefly visit with Tabina and Banner while on the third level. They reconfirmed their plans for later that evening and reassured each other that things would be alright. Everything would be fine once they left the Calming Quarters. But again, none of them were thinking beyond leaving the confines of the building. Where they were going or what they would do, once they escaped, was still a vague concept with no definite strategies or plan. By dinner hour they had managed to empty three of the trolleys and were ravenous by that time. The temptation to stop and have dinner was great, but since the last trolley was still down at the laundry room level, they thought better than leave it there. They pushed the trolley to the next level up and continued the monotonous chore of putting linen onto shelves and drawers. On their last trip to the trolley, for the remaining armload of linen, they noticed a healing assistant heading in their direction. They were weary with the constant walking, bending and stooping and dreaded what they were going to be accosted with this time. There was no escape from her determined purpose: she stopped right in front of them.

"Don't you think you have worked hard enough already?" came a very pleasant and gentle voice in front of them. They looked up and met the glance of beautiful, huge, deep golden eyes with black edging around the iris. They were like pools of a tropical ocean with night closing in. They looked at her face and recognized the kind healing assistant that they had encountered earlier. She glanced briefly at them both but her eyes kept coming back to Raeban. It was like she couldn't help herself. She couldn't look away. Raeban hadn't really noticed anything out of the ordinary but Meeyha could sense that the healing assistant was disconcerted. She reluctantly came to herself and continued in the same kind voice, "dinner is almost over, if you hurry you can just get something to eat before they clean everything up."

Meeyha looked at her armload of linen and then to Raeban's. She was just about to say that they weren't finished when the healing assistant gently took the linen out of Meeyha's arms and replaced them on the trolley. She turned and did the same with Raeban's. "I'll finish up for you. You won't be able to work at all if you don't get something to eat first." With that she gave them each a warm smile and proceeded to place the linens back on the trolley shelves. They gave her a heartfelt thank you and went off to find the dining room. Once they were finished eating they again headed for the back door. This time no one detained them as they slyly slipped out the back door of the Calming Quarters and into the dimly lit profusion of shrubs, trees and flowers. As Meeyha followed Raeban she was hoping that no one noticed their white jobbers' tunics. They had forgotten to leave them behind but they couldn't go back in again for fear of being noticed. They hesitated momentarily, looking for the most suitable hiding place, before they ran along the grass in the emerging twilight.

They assessed their options, then they noticed a couple of people standing by the monument with their backs to the building. The man and woman were carrying on a slightly animated conversation, as if discussing the monument in front of them. They were so engrossed in their discussion that they didn't notice Meeyha's and Raeban's speedy exit from the building. Raeban's goal now was the grouping of three huge rose bushes, to the side of the building, where their view would be clear to the building, the back of the yard and the breezeway to the Potting Shed but still obscuring their presence from anyone casually looking around. As they hunkered down into the bushy plants Raeban's sleeve caught one of the sharp, long thorns growing from the rose's trunk. It made a small ripping sound as Raeban pulled sharply away from the throne. Meeyha grabbed Raeban and pulled him down closer to the ground. They were far enough away from the two at the monument that they may not have heard the sound, but Meeyha didn't want to chance anyone spotting them when they were so close to completing the most important mission in their short lives. They remained crouched for a few seconds then gingerly and silently pulled the leaves apart and peeked out towards the monument. The pair was gone. Meeyha and Raeban frantically looked around to see if their hideaway had been compromised but found no one. There didn't appear to have been enough time for the couple to come back into the building, or go past them towards the 'Potting Shed'. The only two options, as it appeared to Meeyha and Raeban, was either the tunnel which connected to the Cleansing Quarters or around the opposite side of the building that would lead to the front of the building. They had no way to know for sure, so they could only sit where they were and wait. Of course, they didn't have any other plan so they let fate carry them where it would.

As the light began to fade further, Meeyha and Raeban adjusted their position to make their wait a little more comfortable. No one else had appeared since the two had disappeared so Meeyha and Raeban felt secure in their temporary shelter. They even started to discuss their predicament in very soft whispers interspersed with glances behind them and every direction from which they could possibly be discovered. Meeyha commented first, "just lucky we forgot to leave the white tunics behind, otherwise our arms would be cut up and bleeding all over."

"You're right there but more important, was our presence discovered or were those two discussing something else. You know they were waiting for two other jobbers when that healing assistant in training found us. But, since we lasted the whole day in there, we may have been taken as the real jobbers. So what happened to the other jobbers that were expected? Well, no matter, as long as Tabina and Banner are able to meet us as planned. I guess we just wait here until 2200 hours, I guess in about two hours, then we take Tabina and Banner back through the tunnel with us. If that conveyance is still there we can see if we can get it working and get out of this place." Raeban finally stopped talking. He wasn't sure that would be the best course of action, but since they hadn't discussed anything else he hoped it would work for them.

Meeyha thought for a few minutes about what Raeban had said then presented her take on the situation, "That sounds like a possibility, but—". Before Meeyha could finish her dialogue, she spotted the two, who had been talking near the monument earlier, reappear from the other side of the building and head right for the rose bushes. Meeyha held her breath as she motioned Raeban to be quiet with her index finger over her lips with one hand and the other pointing through the leaves towards the two approaching the rose bushes. As the pair stood in front of the rose bushes, barely two feet from where Meeyha and Raeban crouched, they began to whisper, all the while earnestly looking around them. Meeyha was the closest to the pair but she still had to strain to hear what they were saying. As she listened, Meeyha peeked through the leaves and was astounded by what she saw and heard.

One of the healing assistants, who had given instructions to Meeyha and Raeban that morning outside the operating room, was in deep conversation with the Surgical Master who had just completed a procedure, when Meeyha and Raeban arrived as the two jobbers. "That's what I said, the Master of Masters is coming here tonight. He thinks there's a couple wandering around here and that they may be on to what we're doing. He wants us to see if they're still here and if so he wants us to keep them here, sedate them but don't hurt them. He wants to talk to them himself. He also wants to know if the older couple, a revered, retired, Level Three Master and The Keeper of the Archives, have turned up yet. None of us here have seen them yet, but then they're so old they probably forgot all about what they were supposed to do." She laughed unkindly at her attempt at a joke.

"I wouldn't be too quick to write the older couple off. If you think that their minds are going just because they are old, then think again. The Keeper of the Archives is responsible for recording and keeping all that happens in the Compound safe and secure, and the old Level Three Master is just one level below the Master of Masters himself. He knows more than the two of us put together." The chastisement had been delivered as kindly and as non-disparagingly as was possible, but the healing assistant none-the-less felt the sting of the reproach. She remained quiet as the Surgical Master continued. "Let's just have a look around back here first then go inside and lock the doors. If they are here we'll find them. But before anybody is sedated, I'd like to talk to them myself."

With that, the two moved away from the rose bushes and proceeded to look behind large trees and clustered lawn furniture and then finally behind the monument. It looked like they even peeked into the tunnel but did not enter. Meeyha and Raeban finally realized that they had been holding their breaths and almost chocked as they tried to bring their breathing back to normal. As they walked past the rose bushes they made to look behind the bushes but then just peeked on either side. Meeyha and Raeban had had the presence to remove their stark, white tunics as they watched their pursuers look around the backyard, otherwise as the pair had glanced from the sides, they would have seen the terrified couple hunkering down along the grass and leaves under the rose bushes. However, the dark brown everyday tunics that Meeyha and Raeban wore blended in with the earth that surrounded the rose bushes. What they looked like with their heads tucked under the leaves and arms and legs wound around the bushes, were two mounds of earth heaped along the back of the rose bushes. If the night had been any brighter, though, the folds of their tunics might have been seen for what they were. Thankfully Meeyha and Raeban remained still, with their faces in the dirt and again holding their breaths, as the healing assistant and the Surgical

Master glanced around, then moved on. They entered the Calming Quarters and Meeyha and Raeban could hear the bolt settle into place as the door was locked securely from the inside. With their faces still in the dirt, Meeyha and Raeban moved ever so slightly to be able to breath but remained where they were for a few minutes. There were no windows in the door but there were windows from other rooms at the back of the building so they waited until they thought it was safe enough to emerge from the dirt and leaves.

"Wow, that was close" whispered Raeban as he lifted his head from the dirt then gently tapped Meeyha. "I'm fine" replied Meeyha as she tried to remove the dirt from her face and hair. "Let's move back towards the monument so we can talk," continued Meeyha. Raeban took her hand, scooped up the two white tunics from underneath them and ran, hiding behind shrubs, then trees, then flowers as they made their way to the monument. They crouched down behind the monument but didn't approach the tunnel entrance. For all they knew, there may be person or persons coming through the tunnel now. They tried to make themselves as inconspicuous as possible as they waited. It was imperative that they discuss their options but they needed to keep their voices as low as possible so that they could hear any noise around them but yet they themselves would not be heard. Meeyha tried to begin where she had left off, when the healing assistant and the Surgical Master had reappeared, "About your plan to get out of here: I think we need to—" Raeban abruptly put his hand over Meeyha's mouth and turned her to face the back of the building.

Meeyha resisted against Raeban's hand but finally realized that someone had come into the backyard and was walking towards the monument where they were hiding. It was the healing assistant that had finished off their chore and sent them off for their dinner. Meeyha motioned to Raeban that she understood what was happening. She, very quietly whispered directly into Raeban's ear who the healing assistant was and that she felt that this healing assistant was no threat to them. But as they silently watched her from their vantage point they noticed that she just sat at one of the lawn tables and chairs that were spread around the yard. As she sat down she looked briefly around her and took a small piece of paper and placed it in between the cracks on the top of the table. She sat for a moment longer then calmly got up and walked back to the Calming Quarters. Meeyha and Raeban watched until she disappeared around the corner then Raeban motioned to Meeyha that he would retrieve the piece of paper and warily headed across the short distance to where the table was. He plucked the piece of paper from the table and made his way back to the monument.

Meeyha moved slightly away from the monument, as Raeban returned, and as she neared the concealed entrance to the tunnel, her foot kicked a hard object against the tunnel wall. The noise was deafening in the quiet backyard, and Meeyha and Raeban both froze in their tracks and slowly melted into the ground. They remained in that position for a while, then not hearing anyone coming to investigate the sound, they got up and Meeyha explained what had happened to Raeban. The note had been momentarily forgotten as they both searched the ground for the hard object that Meeyha had accidentally kicked as she moved. Raeban then spotted a small blue light emitting from under a small grouping of flowers. As he reached down to pick it up it started to vibrate against his hand. Startled, he withdrew his hand than realized it was someone's personal communicator. To his amazement he recognized his own communicator, which he hadn't even missed. He seized the communicator and fanatically examined the communication being transmitted. He had prudently programmed it to silent mode when they had started out that morning, then must have dropped it when he crawled out of the tunnel.

"Meeyha," Raeban creped over to where she waited, "it was just my communicator. I must have dropped it earlier and guess what: there's a message from White." His voice excitedly grew louder at the last comment. She shushed him and moved closer to study the communicator for herself. "Raeban wait a second, what was that piece of paper?" Raeban pulled the piece of paper from his pocket and gingerly unfolded the small note. Meeyha and Raeban sat close to each other and, by the small light emitting from Raeban's communicator, read the note. 'MASTER OF MASTERS TO INSPECT PROGENY—POSSIBLE PURGING REQUIRED—IGNOMINY SUSPECTED.'

Meeyha and Raeban looked at each other, neither comprehending the words on the note. It could have been a note to herself about what was expected with the Master of Masters' visit but why would she have put it so deliberately in the crack then walk away? Raeban looked at Meeyha and asked, "What is that supposed to mean, and who IS she?" Meeyha thought a moment then answered the first question but withheld, what she believed, about the other, "Raeban she was helping us: she is warning us. Maybe the Master of Masters knows what we are planning and she wants us to be aware." Raeban's eyes shot wide open, then he looked down at the soundless communicator in his hand. He activated the communication and they both listened to White's anxious message. "Raeban, Meeyha, I'm at the Cleansing Quarters with The Keeper of the Archives. There's too much to explain now, but we think that you are in some kind of trouble, maybe even danger. Please contact me as soon as you get this. We need to talk immediately!" Raeban looked at Meeyha and stated the obvious; "I think things are going to get really bad. I hope morning finds us all alive somewhere." Meeyha just looked at him, big tears welling up in her eyes. They sat on the cold ground, darkness all around and hugged each other for a long time. Eventually the strain, excitement, terror and apprehension of the day had left them drained of all energy in body and mind. Their subconscious took over and they fell into an uneasy sleep, there on the cold ground behind the monument, with evil waiting to ensnare them.

Even before Meeyha's eyes closed, the images began to appear behind her eye lids. It was like a movie scene was being projected directly onto her lids, they were so clear and vibrant. She could see both herself and Raeban on the ground, just as they sat hugging each other, with their backs against the cold, hard surface of the monument's base. Their arms still around each other, just as they had been when they fell into the strange state of suspension. But the dream was different though. It was daylight, with the brightest day that she had ever experienced, the sun so bright that she had to avert her paining eyes. Then the bright light became a small bird as it flew over their heads and onto the monument. It was the same small bird that she had rescued: how long ago? It seemed ages. But the small bird wasn't the same either. It appeared larger and more regal. His feathers were a beautiful, translucent white which seemed to emit the brightness that she thought was the sun. She stared at the bird, all the while the bird was looking down at her from his perch on the arm of the monument of the child. It opened its beak and strange words sounded, instead of the expected chirping or bird calls. It said: "We are trapped between this world and the next. Help us reach our final rest." With that Meeyha slowly reopened her eyes and there was the same small bird flying over their heads and then landed on the child's arm. Just like in her dream. However it was night now and very dark. How could that small bird have been flying in the dark: and from where? He was different than in her dream though: his feathers were again the same pure white that she remembered when she had rescued him. And this time he didn't look at her. He looked beyond her and Raeban, as if he was watching something in the distance. Meeyha turned instinctively in the same direction but all she could see was the dark night. Then Raeban, sensing Meeyha's movements, opened his eyes. "Meeyha," he whispered, "what's the matter? Did you hear something?"

"No, Raeban. Look, there's the little bird from the other day." And, as she pointed up at the bird where he was perched, he opened his beautiful wings and flew towards the Calming Quarters and disappeared. Raeban and Meeyha fell silent as they contemplated what they had seen. This was most unusual but they were at a loss to explain it. Song birds don't fly around in the dark. So what was happening? Again, another question with no answer: then he glanced at his timepiece. It showed 2100 hours. One hour before their planned meeting with Tabina and Banner. Well, maybe they should try to sleep again, the sleep would help clear their heads and give them the energy they needed to deal with the next phase of their adventure. But instead of trying to fall asleep Raeban turned to Meeyha and whispered in her ear. She had been trying to tell him something when they had left the Calming Quarters and they were interrupted each time she started telling him. "Meeyha, what were you trying to tell me before?" He looked at her as she sat, eyes wide open, staring out into the wooded area, now totally black. "Raeban, I was thinking that we should take Tabina and Banner, once we get them out of the Calming Quarters, and wait in the trees until we can get in touch with White and let him know what we have found out. Maybe he can help us think this through properly and then no one will get hurt. And since we found your communicator, and we know that he is already here, or at least at the Cleansing Quarters, he'll certainly be able to help us. Try sending him another message. Maybe he'll answer this time." She finished talking and turned to Raeban, pleading with her eyes. She didn't want anyone to be hurt, least of all those that she had grown to love and care for. She knew that their lives in the compound had changed forever but she still hoped that whatever went wrong could be resolved with care and compassion for everyone involved. Raeban took her silence to be expectation so he took his communicator and proceeded to send another message to White. As expected Raeban's attempt to reach White had failed again but he was still able to leave a message that White would, hopefully, discover later.

It was almost time to head back to the Calming Quarters but both Meeyha and Raeban had their doubts that things would go as they expected. With the untimely appearance of the Master of Masters their hopes of a clean escape were looking very slim. But in spite of the odds against them they were determined not to let Tabina and Banner down. They would do the best they could to at least get them out of the building so that they would be able to talk to them again, without constantly looking over their shoulder expecting someone to appear and discover their presence and their hidden agendas. They crept slowly from flowers to trees to shrubs until they reached the rose bush that they had hidden behind when they left the building. Everything was silent as they reached the building. There were no visible movements outside, and from what they could see through the windows, there was no one moving inside. Raeban left Meeyha behind the rose bush and tried to edge as close as he dared to the back door. He tried the door, but just as he feared it was still locked. Worst still he had no way to find out if Tabina and Banner had been able to leave their room. The best thing would be to wait for awhile, if they were able to leave then they would be there, but it was more likely that they could not leave. Raeban made his way, quickly and quietly, back to where Meeyha was waiting.

"Meeyha, the door's locked; what do you think? Should we wait here or try getting into the building some other way?" Raeban valued Meeyha's judgement and this was important enough for them both to consider it properly. The consequences could be immense.

"Why don't we try to get in through the Potting Shed." Suggested Meeyha.

"What do you mean, the Potting Shed?" Queried Raeban.

"I mean that there is another entrance to the Potting Shed. Well, at least I think there is. Remember when we first got here and you went to check out the Calming Quarters and I waited at the monument? Well that caretaker, gardener or whatever he is, came from the direction of the bridge to the monument then back the same way. There must be an entrance there. Why don't we try that?" Meeyha hoped that she was right. If not they would be exposing themselves to anyone coming or going inside that glass bridge.

"Alright, let's go" agreed Raeban. They had to do something, and that seemed like a good option. They started to step out from behind the rose bushes when the back door opened a crack. They hurriedly scooted back under the bushes, cutting their arms and hands on the sharp thorns. There was no way that they could see who it was at the door. Maybe it was Tabina, but then again it could be someone else. They didn't know what to do. The only thing they could do was stay where they were and hope for the best. As far as they could tell, no one came out of the building but they could hear the door quietly close again. Holding their breath, they inched their heads up to peek through the leaves. It was dark enough that they wouldn't be noticed immediately, if there was someone out there to take notice, but not light enough for them to pick out any human form. They waited a few more minutes, then Raeban whispered into Meeyha's ear that he would go try the door again to see if it was unlocked. Meeyha grabbed his arm and urgently whispered back. "Please be careful!" Raeban nodded, gave her a reassuring smile and slithered back towards the door. He carefully reached up to try the door knob again. Slowly he turned the knob. But again he met resistance. It was locked again. Who could have looked out the door then go back inside if not Tabina? Whoever it was, what or who were they looking for? Raeban hoped they weren't looking for them.

"Guess, we try our alternate option. The door's locked again." Raeban whispered to Meeyha once he got back to her behind the rose bush. Meeyha nodded and whispered, "Well, let's go." Raeban rose and ran ahead, in a bent crouch, with Meeyha close behind. It was just a few minutes to reach the back side of the Potting Shed, and just as Meeyha had suspected, there was a door into the small building. There was also a window in the door and they peeked inside before attempting to open it. Since there was no light emanating from the window, they knew there was no light on inside but cautiously looked in just the same. There didn't appear to be anyone around so Raeban tried the door. To their surprise, the door knob turned easily in Raeban's hand, he opened it just wide enough to allow their admittance. This part of the building only housed what one would expect in a gardener's shed: shovels, old pots, watering cans, a collection of boxes lined up neatly on the shelves on each side of the building and big rubber boots, that must belong to the man Meeyha had seen. They continued past the gardener's paraphernalia and tried the inside door. The door knob turned easily but the door itself gave some resistance. Since this door didn't have a window Raeban carefully gave a slight push and opened the door a crack. Light shone through the crack and the sound of voices could be heard coming from a short distance away.

"Make sure these bodies are disposed of as soon as possible" Raeban and Meeyha looked at each other as they heard someone give instructions to someone in the room, "then go back and put that room back in order. No need to get anyone else involved in this."

"Yes Master Svene" was all the other person said. Then foot steps could be heard as one of them walked away. They assumed the one called Master Svene had been the one to walk away. Just then Meeyha and Raeban both realized who Master Svene was. It was the Master of Masters himself. Of course they already knew that he was there but now they could only think the worst. He must have come to have Tabina and Banner killed and that horrible man, the gardener, was going to make plant food out of them.

Meeyha began to shiver. Raeban swiftly put his arm around her to comfort her and help her suppress the impending sobs. Meeyha calmed herself and dried her eyes with her hands. "Don't jump to conclusions," Raeban whispered "we don't know for sure its Tabina and Banner in there." Meeyha nodded, pale and trembling, standing helplessly in the back of the Potting Shed with boxes of human remains neatly stored along the shelf above their heads. Her resolve again began to falter. There had been nothing in their existence that could have even prepared them for this but that may have worked in their favour. If conscious that something sinister is about to happen one may prepare for the wrong outcome. But with spontaneous occurrences, self-preservation is more than likely to lead to a more favourable outcome. For Meeyha and Raeban, this was their present hope.

As they watched through the crack in the door, they noticed that the gardener pushed the stretchers to the side of the room and then said, "I guess you two aren't going anywhere now. You'll keep until morning, I'm going home to bed." The corpses didn't answer. No one answered and no one was there to mourn the two who had curiously died that evening.

The gardener then turned and headed for the door. Meeyha and Raeban were still watching as his hand reached for the door knob. They were both drawn side ways, away from the opening, as the door was forcibly opened and a beautiful white bird shot past, almost hitting the gardener in the head, as it flew towards the outside door. Meeyha and Raeban watched as the gardener shook his head and proceeded to the outside door, muttering to himself, "Those birds are getting bigger and bigger around here." Then to the disappearing bird outside, "Don't know how you got in here but I'll make sure you never do, if I see you again." Then he followed the bird out and closed the door behind him; totally unaware of the two listening and watching the proceedings.

Meeyha and Raeban looked around then felt safe enough to enter the inside room. This was where the corpses were reduced to ashes. There was what looked like a big table with sides around the perimeter of the table top. Above that was a cone shaped piece of equipment directed towards the top of the table. It could be moved back and forth over the table as well as side to side. They were repulsed as they imagined what happened on that table. Meeyha pulled Raeban away, she couldn't bear the thoughts any longer. "Raeban, I want to see who is under the sheets." She quietly implored him. "I need to know if it's Tabina and Banner on those stretchers."

"Meeyha, I'll look; please don't worry." Raeban tried to reassure her but felt very inadequate. He pulled one of the sheets up and looked briefly at what it covered. Then he moved to the next stretcher and did the same. He turned to the anxiously waiting Meeyha and said, "It's not Tabina and Banner" his voice not revealing what he had just witnessed. But Meeyha persisted with her questions. "But who is it then, Raeban?" She believed him, but she was still uneasy with the look on his face. "Meeyha, let it be. It's not Tabina and Banner, for now that's all we can worry about." Raeban's voice sounded nervous and strained, but he wasn't going to let Meeyha look at the corpses. He didn't know what else would befall them that evening and he didn't want Meeyha to breakdown and jeopardize their escape.

He gently pulled her behind him as he quietly pushed the door opening into the glass bridge. The floral scent filled their nostrils as they cautiously stepped into the bridge. They both subconsciously shivered as they envisioned the plants being nourished by the gardener. But they pushed the unpleasant thoughts out of the heads and made their way into the Calming Quarters. Once inside the main building again, fear began to crept into their blood. They were lucky the day before, no one had questioned their identity or their presence, but now, with the Master of Masters here and looking for them, they were going to have to be very careful not to be seen by anyone. As they also found out the day before, that was harder than it sounded. There were very few hiding places and even fewer places where there were no people about. Again, they hadn't made any plans; they didn't know what to do first. Should they go see if Tabina and Banner were alright, or should they just get a hold of White and let him deal with the situation.

Well, they were the ones at the Calming Quarters now, and, if they didn't find out about Tabina and Banner while they could, it may be too late if they waited. So their plan evolved as they went along.

Chapter 20

White contemplated what Bianca had just told Viki. He was well aware that there was an outside world and that, for centuries, the inhabitants of the compound had been kept as innocent as babes. But to leave the compound and inform the outside world of their existence, their captive existence, sounded too enormous an endeavour. White had himself thought of doing just that shortly after Coral had passed away. He had been so despondent in those years that he was amazed that he was able to continue on as he had. But then his work was all he had; and even considering what he had been doing, all those years, to all those poor innocents, he had to continue, because it had been a cause that he could lose himself in. And he had done just that; until he began to see what the true effects of those 'adjustments' had been to them all. They were humans still, but to be human was to have all the emotions and feelings that went along with being human. Humans weren't ever perfect but that was what the founding fathers had wanted to create, when they conceived the notion back then; perfect human beings that would carry their dreams to fruition. The dreams of no more wars, no more hunger, no more pollution and even to the extent of no more natural disasters, that destroyed so much human life, let alone all the other living things. Natural disasters had been impossible to control: in spite of all the satellites launched into space to try to manipulate the earth's magnetic fields and solar flares that threatened the entire earth. Nature had a way of doing what it wanted, no permission requested. Yet the founding fathers let themselves think that they could do all that, and they convinced everyone that came after them that it was happening. But did the founding fathers even have any notion of how much their cause would deviate from the original ideas? When had the dome become their entire world, with never a word about what was to become of them under that dome? Why had it been necessary to keep everyone so ignorant of the true nature of their existence under that dome?

He couldn't answer any of those questions. Maybe no one would ever be able to answer them. The present Masters, including himself, had allowed those founding fathers to try to recreate a perfect world for their supposed perfect human beings. But none of the Masters had ever thought to question the value of their cause. And now there was no one that could set these poor damaged human beings back into the life that they had been meant to lead. Imperfect? Definitely. Violent? Probably always. Doomed to destruction? Never, at least not by humanity's doing, they had already proved that. Fighting amongst certain factions would always exist, but the will to live was still very strong in the majority and that majority would always persist with ways to avert total annihilation. White was as sure of that as he was sure that he would do everything in his power to help those kids trying to bring the real human qualities back into their existence.

The kids these days; they were getting more brazen than ever. Who could they possibly confide in, in the outside world, that would take any interest in 'rescuing' a strange band of people from an imagined captivity. The compound had been protected from the outside world for so long that it was very unlikely that any, in the outside world, would even be aware of their existence. But, by all that was good and great in their imperfect world, White would do whatever he could to help bring a stop to all the atrocities going on at the Calming Quarters.

White was exhausted. He hadn't been this emotional since Coral had died. But now he was no longer despondent. Things were going to be right again. He longed to experience all that was out there to experience; the rain for one. It would be wonderful to feel the warm rain falling on his head from the heavens. He had read all about the rain and the wind and the sun beating down on bare skin and he looked forward to feeling it all.

"Yes, we'll do it!" White almost shouted at Viki. Bianca nearly jumped out of her skin. White had not been so expressive, not even when he was younger. Well, at least not that she could remember.

Viki went to White and through her arms around White and hugged him with all her strength. She was so relieved tears started falling of their own accord. She released him and wiped her tears away embarrassed to have shown such emotion. This was a surprise, even to herself. White looked at her again, this time he really looked at her. To his astonishment, the thoughts that this young lady could be related to him, immediately came into his head. She could be his niece, or a distant cousin even. Now, more than ever, he longed to see Meeyha and Raeban; to make sure that they were safe. He thought of his communicator and decided he would send them another message. It was imperative that he get through as soon as possible. He didn't know exactly how to say everything that had coursed through his brain in the last few minutes. If he tried it would probably take an hour to make Raeban understand what he himself still was trying to digest. But in the end he made it as short and as meaningful as he was able. He began with a calm voice and spoke into his communicator "HUMANITY WAS CONCEIVED IN LOVE AND CONCERN; BUT EVOLVED AS DICTATED BY MAN; NOW WE MAY DIE BUT WE WILL DIE AS FREE AND INDEPENDENT BEINGS. Please contact me immediately; The Keeper of the Archives, and I have very urgent news for you. And remember, you and Meeyha have come to mean more to me than my own life. Please, please contact me immediately."

White felt drained. It was like the last few minutes had taken the greatest toll on his life. He was beyond understanding all these emotions but it was enormously better than living without any emotions at all. For so many years his life had been a constant routine with little or no true emotional contact with anything or anyone: except of course, when Coral was in his life. Now it was like he had found his family and he would do anything to keep them safe and close to his heart. Then he took his communicator and sent another message. Eventually one of them must get through to them. Now they must try to find their way to the Calming Quarters and find out what was going on in there. Viki had mentioned the tunnel that connected the Cleansing Quarters with the Calming Quarters. Then that was how he and Bianca were going to get there. Viki had produced another small light that would guide them through the darkness. The night itself was very dark, and the tunnel would be darker still if that were possible. He hoped neither he nor Bianca were claustrophobic, otherwise they may never get out of that tunnel. But no time to worry about anything other than getting to the Calming Quarters before something terrible happened.

Viki lead them to the tunnel entrance and explained how to operate the doors into the tunnel and everything else that they would need to know to get them safely to the Calming Quarters. Then she gave White and Bianca a final hug and bid them a safe undertaking. She would try to see if Valtre could do anything about getting the communicators back in operation. "White," Viki said, "make sure you keep your communicator on silent mode. There's no telling who may be lurking around there at night. Although, the healing assistants do take a few hours rest during the quiet hours but with all the goings on, the routine may have changed now. Good luck, and stay safe."

White took Bianca's hand and they proceeded as instructed into the tunnel. The blackness was almost suffocating, then very slowly a strange soft glow started emitting from the tunnel walls. White whispered to Bianca that he thought there must be glow worms in the tunnel that were giving off that faint glow. Whatever it was, it was a welcome sight to them both.

Chapter 21

Once Meeyha and Raeban had entered the Calming Quarters they knew that they couldn't turn back. They were now totally committed, no matter what was going to happen. The hall was empty as they crept silently towards the laundry room, it seemed to be the best place to hide in while they tried to think through what they should do. Luck was with them for Master Svene and his helper were no where in sight. There weren't any sounds or voices audible at all, so they continued till they reached the laundry room door. The wide double door was closed but opened noisily when Raeban gave it a small push. They held their breath as they waited to see if anyone would come to investigate the sound. No one came so they inched their way through the small opening that Raeban had made and slowly closed the door behind them. Just as it came to a final stop it gave a high squeal that must have carried to the higher levels. Spurred on by fear they spotted a tall trolley loaded with clean linen. Without thinking any further they scurried behind the trolley and waited. To their disappointment they heard steps and the double doors were flung open.

What were they thinking? Behind the trolley would be the first place they looked: they waited as still and quiet as statues. Now all was quiet. And no one said a word. Meeyha and Raeban had heard multiple foot steps. There were probably two or three people out there but no one was saying anything. The suspense was killing Meeyha and Raeban. They had held their breath when the door opened and now they were afraid to start breathing for fear of giving themselves away. Then the foot steps moved into the room. They appeared to be going in different directions but one set was definitely coming their way. As they waited, almost faint with lack of oxygen, they saw a shadow come close to the trolley. To their surprise they heard a voice, only loud enough for them to hear but the message was unmistakable.

"Stay where you are and don't move a muscle."

Meeyha and Raeban could feel their world shatter around them. It was like a physical force, the knowledge that they would soon die. And not just them but the others that they had tried so hard to protect. Raeban took hold of his courage and peered around the end of the trolley. The person who had given them the scare of their lives was facing away from them. Her back was to them. Had she talked to them or someone else in the room? It must have been them, there was no one else in the room besides them.

"Master Svene, why don't we separate and each search a different area. We'll be done sooner and if there is anyone in here then they have to pass one of us to get out." The speaker was the same one that had told them to stay put, but this time it was a little louder to project to the other side of the room. "Of course Essa, that would be best. I'll leave the two of you to look through the rest of the laundry room. I'll check the potting shed, they likely were going out of the laundry room rather than coming in." His voice faded at he turned and opened the laundry room double doors, then left.

The lady named Essa then spoke to the other person in the room. "I'll look through this soiled linen, if that is alright with you, and you can check the clean linen in other room. I'll make sure this trolley over here is clear."

The other then answered Essa with a definite; "That suits me just fine. There's no way I'm going near that dirty stuff!" Then his foot steps faded as he went into the other room. Meeyha and Raeban waited. Essa watched the Master's bodyguard as he went into the clean linen storage room then quietly whispered to the two hiding behind the trolley. It was just a few steps behind where Essa stood so she turned and called quietly for the two to come out. Having regained their composure, Meeyha and Raeban filed slowly from behind the trolley. They all gasped in surprise as they recognized who each other were. Essa's eyes particularly widened in surprise and her heart started racing in her breast. She was pleased to see them again, but she would have wished that it had been under different circumstances. "You must hurry and leave here, you are in grave danger if Master Svene finds you here" she spoke quickly, now furtively looking to see if the bodyguard was within hearing distance. The coast was still clear but not for too much longer. Raeban opened his mouth to protest, but Essa motioned them to be quiet again and ushered them back behind the trolley.

"You were right, there's no one here now. Those two probably left the laundry room to leave the building not hiding to stay inside. Master Svene has probably already caught them. Let's go see." The bodyguard started for the double doors expecting to see Essa close behind him. As he opened the door to let her pass he noticed that she hadn't moved from her position next to the trolley. Essa had to quickly come up with an excuse not to go with him. She looked at him with concern and innocently said, "But they could be dangerous for just Master Svene alone, shouldn't we get more help?"

"No" retorted the bodyguard, "those two are just kids, they aren't dangerous themselves. Master Svene just doesn't like people wandering around where they have no business being."

"Oh," remarked Essa, "in that case then why don't you go on ahead and I'll go back upstairs and continue my normal routine. You know it's almost time for the healing assistants to go for their sleep and everyone has to be sedated before that. I'll lock these doors from the outside, since we've already thoroughly checked inside and found no one, then I'll bring the key with me and keep it safe."

"Well, if that's what you want I don't think Master Svene will mind. You just happened to be the only one available to come down here with us, so you weren't that vital to the search. Go ahead then I'll wait till you lock the doors." And with that he stood nearby while Essa locked Meeyha and Raeban inside the laundry room: now again unable to reach Tabina and Banner.

Essa's mind was racing as she used slow deliberate moves to lock the doors, but try as she might she couldn't think of anything else to do but leave the two trapped in the laundry room. The key was needed to unlock the doors from the inside but there was no way that she could leave it for them now. She decided that she would have to come back down and let them out later when everyone was asleep. The more she thought about that, the better she felt. If they were confined in a safe place they couldn't be hurt or get themselves into anymore trouble. She would be down in about another hour and let them out, then she could find out what exactly they were doing here and why the Master of Masters himself had to come down to see to their capture.

Meeyha and Raeban listened to Essa and the bodyguard as they discussed the situation. They had hoped that Essa would leave the door unlocked so they could continue their mission, but now all they could do was wait down here until she came back. At least they hoped that she would come back. She didn't seem to want to give their presence away, so she must be wanting to help them. They made themselves comfortable behind the trolley and Raeban took out his communicator to check for a response from White. Still nothing. It was now close to 2300 hours. If Tabina and Banner were waiting, as planned, they must be terrified: thought Raeban. But there was absolutely nothing they could do now. Maybe if they looked around they might be able to find another way out of here. But then what if Essa came back and they were gone, what would she do then. Surly she wouldn't tell anyone about their escape. No, Raeban thought not, so he gave Meeyha a tap and told her about his plan. Together they opened every door, looked for any accessible window, but found none at all, then checked every ceiling and floor for possible trap doors. But there was absolutely nothing that they could use to make their escape. They resigned themselves to wait for Essa to return.

After Master Svene had left the laundry room he headed directly to the Potting Shed. When he entered he was surprised to see that the two cadavers were still there. Not wanting to have corpses just out in the open he decided to take care of the corpses himself, but Master Svene was certainly going to talk to the gardener when he saw him the next day. No one ignored his orders, especially the gardener at the Calming Quarters. He should have known better than to leave cadavers lying around for all to see. Things like this should be attended to immediately. There were no living beings in here, as far as Master Svene could see, so he proceeded to make the preparations for disposal of the corpses. He noticed that the equipment was ancient, as he started to initiate the sequence, and that it was taking longer than normal to reach disintegration power. He gave the controls a second adjustment then the brilliant, searing power of the laser infused the entire potting shed: the deed was done.

Master Svene turned to leave the potting shed but as he turned he noticed a white feather slowly floating down to the floor. He watched it for a few seconds then looked around for the bird that must surely be somewhere in the room. But there was no bird in sight. On a whim, he picked up the feather. It was probably a flight feather for it was long and strong. The feel of the feather gave him a warm, nostalgic feeling. He shook his head as if to disperse the thoughts that the feather elicited. He longed for his family and his children on the other side. His two boys had wanted a bird and so he had conceded and purchased them a beautiful cock-a-too with feathers the same colour as the one he held in his hand. He continued out of the potting shed: his thoughts miles away.

Chapter 22

Essa was able to return to her duties with little notice from her colleagues, not that anyone would ever make any comments about someone's activities, but now Essa had a reason to be unobtrusive. She wanted to get back to the two kids locked in the laundry room without anyone being the wiser. So she went about her work as quickly and as efficiently as possible. Finally, the time came that all the patients had been checked and sedated for the night. Now the healing assistants themselves could take a few hours rest before preparing for the morning routine.

Living right on the Calming Quarters premises was a conundrum: it was great because the healing assistants didn't have to trudge back and forth daily to and from their quarters, but then they also didn't have the down time between shifts when they could relax and do nothing. But for Essa, she was thankful that the Masters at the Calming Quarters had made the decision for them; although none of the healing assistants would have made any complaint: this served her purpose well on this particular night. Essa put together a few sandwiches and some fruit juices for the kids downstairs: funny she didn't even know the kids' names but she felt totally protective of them, especially the young man. Essa wanted to find out more about them but the opportunity hadn't presented itself and now probably wouldn't, considering the situation. She put that notion in the back of her head and proceeded with her mission.

Once everyone had dispersed to their own sleeping quarters, Essa hurried back down to the laundry room. As she went down the stairs she thought of Master Svene and hoped that he had left the Calming Quarters for his own quarters at the Cleansing Quarters. When she reached the landing that continued to the back door of the Calming Quarters she heard foot steps on the lower level coming towards the stairs. As she rounded the staircase she noticed Master Svene continuing straight to the laundry room doors. Her heart skipped a beat when she saw him try the handles. But since she had locked the doors earlier he could not gain entrance. He appeared unfazed and turned to go up the stairs now directly in front of Essa. She started to descend again trying to appear calm and nonchalant carrying the tray with sandwiches and juice. But he was walking straight with head neither looking around nor turning in any direction. While he walked he stroked a white feather that he held in his hand. He walked right past Essa on the stairs without making any sign of acknowledgment. Essa looked back to see him continue up to the upper level and out the front doors, possibly to the Cleansing Quarters. Essa could hear Master Svene's bodyguard calling after him but again he showed no sign of neither hearing or seeing anyone or anything around him.

At this point, Essa felt it better that she didn't meet up with the bodyguard again so she hurried down the rest of the steps to the laundry room. She hesitated a moment and looked in the opposite direction to the Potting Shed. She was torn between going to see what had transpired in the Potting Shed but then she needed to let the two kids out of the laundry room. There was no choice right now but to go back to the laundry room and the kids. Once inside she closed the doors quietly, fortunately the doors hadn't protested as she had opened them as they had earlier that evening. She looked around for the two. She called softly for them to come out and waited for them to emerge. When they didn't come out she take a few steps towards the trolley behind which they had been hiding earlier. Sure enough there they were, both sound asleep with the girl snuggled in the boys arms. Essa's heart surged with the tender scene before her. She remembered when she had been younger and her partner had held her in that way. But she breathed a wistful sign then gently shook the young man awake.

Raeban opened his eyes and meet the most beautiful pairs of eyes he had even seen, looking straight into his own. There was something very familiar about those eyes and the tilt of her nose. It was almost like looking in the mirror, except that his raven black hair was short while hers' was long and pulled back away from her face. Then the realization hit him. This was the same healing assistant that had helped with the linen trolley and also the same one that had left the note in the table. That must be it. She was helping them not trying to hurt them. Meeyha was right. Then he looked away from Essa and gently tapped Meeyha on her cheek to wake her up. Meeyha opened her eyes and gasped with surprise as she noticed Raeban and Essa watching her.

"I hope I didn't startle you," Essa spoke first then presented the tray with sandwiches and juice, "but I thought you might like something to eat before you leave."

Meeyha and Raeban looked wonder struck. They were amazed at what this woman had done for them already, now here she was with more surprises. And they were glad to see what she had brought for them. Before they began to eat though they needed to find out a few things. Raeban grabbed a sandwich, then as he was unwrapping it, he looked at Essa and asked the question that was foremost in his mind. "Why are you helping us? Wouldn't you get into trouble if you were caught with us? Because I know we are in trouble if the Master of Masters himself is looking for us."

"No," started Essa, "as a matter of fact, something strange just happened when I was coming down here. Master Svene was coming back from the Potting Shed when I was coming down with the tray for the two of you and he passed me on the stairs and neither spoke nor looked at me."

"He didn't see you?" Questioned Meeyha.

"No," began Essa again, "he didn't even make any sign of being aware of my existence. I passed him right on the stairs. Strange though he was holding a white feather in his hand and stroking it all the while. Then he went up, through the front doors and out of the building."

"He's not looking for us anymore?" Raeban asked. "We're free to leave?" He was amazed at the information.

"Well, as far as I can tell Master Svene isn't looking for you but I'm not sure that the bodyguard may not be. But Master Svene walked right past him too and did the same thing. Not a word or glance in his direction." Essa explained as she watched Raeban as he tore into the sandwich. "So, if you two want to go back to the Cleansing Quarters then you are free to go. But before you do I would like to know a little more about the two of you and who you are." As the words left Essa's lips she became uneasy with her request. Absolute strangers don't usually ask such questions of others and she was surprised that she spoke the words out loud. But the young man was so familiar that she wanted to know as much about him as possible.

Then Meeyha surprised them both. "Essa," Meeyha said as she placed her hand on Essa's, "Raeban looks very much like you. He has the same golden eyes and turned up nose and your hair colour is totally identical. Do you think maybe that he is your son?" The last sentence was spoken with such love and gentleness that Essa's eyes filled with warm tears. The tears that had been welling up inside her since the day that they took her first born. From the very first time that she had seen Raeban she had noticed all the similar features, but hadn't wanted to hope too much that her child was here sitting before her, now totally grown, with her never being a part of his life. This had been too much to hope for but her greatest wish had been granted. Now with the knowledge and the presence of her greatest wish, Essa was unable to determine what to do with the knowledge. Essa knew, as did everyone else in the compound, that off spring were given up and forgotten as soon as they were born. But then what is to happen when you meet up with the off spring? She thought for a minute longer then offered her opinions to the young adults before her.

"Yes, I do think that he is my son, but I still think that we should keep that knowledge to ourselves. As long as no one else notices the resemblance we can go about our lives as before. But certainly I would like to be a part of your lives as much as I can." Essa was relieved that she could say that without fear of reprisal. If no one else knew then things could go on as before, but now it was necessary to get them away from here as quickly as possible. Then she realized that she didn't know their names. "By the way my name is Essa but I don't know what your names are."

Meeyha and Raeban were both smiling and the both reached out to hug her, one on either side of her. As their arms linked the tears began to flow from each pair of eyes and the tears mingled together as they fell to the floor. After a few minutes they pulled apart and Meeyha made the introductions, "Essa, this is Raeban and my name is Meeyha. I am so pleased to meet you and I hope that we can be friends forever."

Essa shook each offered hand in turn then threw her arms around Raeban and hugged him close for a very long time. Finally, she let him go but it was with a heavy heart that she thought that she might never see him again after the reunion that they had just shared. Raeban continued looking at her as she pulled herself away from him and he risked voicing the question that now burned within him. "Where is my father now?"

Essa looked down at her hands, new tears forming in her eyes. "Your father was very much against giving you up when you were born." The words came out slow and measured. The next ones she dreaded most to speak. "He was taken away, after he started lashing out at everyone in sight, and I never saw him again." Her tears flowed freely now as she spoke of what she had wanted most to forget. Meeyha put her arms around Essa again but Raeban just looked on still and unresponsive. They stayed there, in the laundry room of the Calming Quarters, a newly found family but now more heavily burdened than moments before.

In the end, Essa was the one to break the silence. "We should get out of here now, before Master Svene regains his presence of mind and comes back after you."

"Wait," sighed Raeban "there are two other people that we came here to find and take away. We almost succeeded but we ran out of time. We were to meet them again tonight but things didn't work out as we had planned. Can you help us get them out?"

"I didn't want to mention this before, but I saw your names on a list of incoming patients." Essa didn't look at them as she said this. She was wishing that what she had just said wasn't true but she had seen the list of "People with Disruptive Tendencies" when she was preparing the present patients for the night. She didn't want to worry them with the knowledge that they were considered 'people with disruptive tendencies', so she asked instead, "Who are the two that you were looking for?" And she hoped that they hadn't been too late to save the two in question.

Meeyha gasped when she digested Essa's words and grabbed Raeban's arm. "Raeban, who were those two in the Potting Shed? Were they Tabina and Banner?" She had started to get frantic again. She couldn't bear that they were in the same building but were unable to get Tabina and Banner out to safety.

Raeban took Meeyha by the shoulders and gently shook her, "I told you, they weren't Tabina and Banner. Those people in the potting shed were NOT Tabina and Banner." Then he took her in his arms and held her close. She sobbed softly for a few minutes then again composed herself and wiped her tears.

"I'm sorry," she said "I don't know what gets into me every so often. It's almost like someone else is pulling me in different directions." She looked at Essa and then at Raeban. They said nothing but Essa looked at Meeyha lovingly and patted her hand.

"We really must get out of here," Essa repeated gently as she stood up. "The healing assistants should all be asleep by now so we can get to your friends and see how we can get the four of you out without anyone seeing you." Essa sounded more confident than she felt. It was true that the healing assistants were asleep but Master Svene's bodyguard was still wandering around the building along with unknown others.

Meeyha and Raeban got up and followed Essa out the door. They looked around for any sign of Master Svene's bodyguard but there was no sign of any one. Essa motioned them towards the elevator. "We'll take the elevator up. Now, what floor are we going to?" She asked as she waved her hand to open the elevator door. "Third floor" called out Raeban as they entered the elevator and headed for the top floor.

When the door opened Essa motioned them to stay back as she stepped forward. A quick glance in every direction assured her that there was no one about. Meeyha and Raeban almost ran out of the elevator when Essa nodded to them. They arrived at Tabina and Banner's room within a few seconds. The door was closed and they looked to Essa to open it. Again Essa looked around then she slowly opened the door. Inside both Tabina and Banner were sound asleep. Meeyha walked to Tabina's bedside and gently shook her shoulder and called her name. To Meeyha's surprise Tabina opened her eyes and smiled at her as she opened her mouth to speak until she noticed Essa standing just inside the door. She quickly closed her eyes and her mouth and remained motionless.

"Tabina," Meeyha said, "it's alright; this is Essa—our friend." She almost said 'Raeban's mother' but she realized that that could wait for another time. Tabina opened her eyes again and spoke very quietly, still cautious. "I'm sorry I couldn't get down to meet you but I couldn't get the pill out of Banner's mouth this time. The healing assistant stayed with him until he swallowed the water. What do we do now?" Meeyha couldn't answer her, she turned to Essa with a silent plea.

Raeban had not moved from his position next to Essa. Then he came forward and answered. "We're leaving. All of us. Now, tonight. This time has to be it." He looked at Essa as he said this then spoke to her in an undertone. "Can you get a stretcher?" Essa nodded and left the room. Raeban turned to Meeyha and Tabina and explained the plan. They were going to use the stretcher to get Banner downstairs. They were going to go through the Potting Shed and out into the back yard. Raeban was going to have to carry Banner from there but he was sure he could make it safely to the tunnel. Even if they had to wait until Banner woke up, they would at least be outside. He hoped that Essa could somehow help them pull off their escape. Raeban looked at his watch. He didn't know how much longer they had before the healing assistants woke up but he wanted to get out as soon as possible. He began to pace as he waited for Essa to return. It had only been a few minutes but to Raeban it seemed like hours since she had left. Then he heard foot steps outside the door. He motioned for Meeyha to hide as he stood beside the door: once opened the door would hide him from view. But the foot steps just went past. Fear and apprehension gripped the three. Banner was oblivious to everything. Raeban thought that he was the lucky one.

Finally, Essa arrived with the stretcher. She apologized for the delay but that she had to go all the way down to the Potting Shed before she locate one, and to her surprise she found two. All the others were being used as temporary beds because there had been an unusual number of patients coming in for treatment during the last few months. Essa explained all this as she helped to ready Banner, with Raeban's help, to be transferred onto the stretcher.

Meeyha looked up when Essa had mentioned the Potting Shed. Then she thought about the two who had occupied the stretchers when she and Raeban had left. She waited until Essa and Raeban were finished transferring Banner onto the stretcher, then she quietly whispered in Essa's ear. "What did you do with the two on the stretchers?" Essa looked at her and said, "There wasn't anyone on either stretcher. They were just inside the Potting Shed, empty." Raeban heard Essa answer Meeyha and then commented himself. "Are you sure there weren't any bodies in the Potting Shed? Because there were a man and a woman on the stretchers when we left."

"Well," Essa thought for a few seconds, "as a matter of fact, there was residue left on the table—uh, that should have been cleared away." She didn't want to tell them that there had been two small ridges of ashes where bodies would have lain once the laser had done its job.

But Raeban persisted, "But I saw them. It was that Surgical master and the healing assistant that were up in the operating room this morning." He looked at Essa with a confused, worried look. "The gardener had left the Potting Shed before we did. We thought for sure he had seen us, but he just walked through to the back room and left." He continued not really asking anybody in particular. "Do you suppose he came back and did the job after we left?"

Essa brought them all back to the present, "No matter who they were and when they were lasered, we just need to get out of here before someone comes along." Essa started to push the stretcher out again but Raeban held her back. "Do you think that Master Svene went and did the job when he left the laundry room?"

"Raeban I don't know, and I don't see why this would affect what we do now." Essa tried to understand what Raeban was leading to.

"Don't you see," Raeban explained, "if Master Svene went to the Potting Shed he must have still been looking for us. He knows that there is a way in from the back room and he had expected us to be running to the Potting Shed to get out, not to be coming inside. And he knew that the Surgical Master and healing assistant were there. He must have sent them there himself, so he decided to finish the job when he didn't find us there. Now I wander if he thinks we're still in here." The last comment gave them all a jolt.

"But Raeban, I saw him leave the building. He was headed back to the Cleansing Quarters: probably to go to bed." Essa tried to make sense of all that had been going on. She knew what happened to people that didn't conform to the expected standards but she didn't think that any of the Masters and healing assistants would just be exterminated especially Surgical Master Raun. He was such a kind and caring man. Essa didn't know who the healing assistant was but she was still shocked with the knowledge that her colleagues were now gone. "Raeban, I'm afraid that Master Svene really means to do all of us harm now. But what do you think we should do?" Essa felt that Raeban should set the course. Since all their lives were in jeopardy if they fell into the Master's hands, Raeban seemed to possess the best instincts with respect to evading the Master's path. She felt confident that he would think of something soon.

"I have an idea" Raeban had been pacing then he stopped. "Essa, you call the Cleansing Quarters and ask to speak to Master Svene. Tell him something urgent came up and that you needed his advice. Then we would know for sure that he was there so we could make our escape. You're going to have to think of something really important but nothing too drastic to make him come running back here—I got it! You can tell him that you needed the Surgical Master but couldn't find him. He wouldn't come back then, since he already knew what had happened to the Surgical Master. What do you think, can you do it?" Raeban was excited now and he wanted to get going.

Essa looked beaten, "Sure Raeban but, I'm sorry, where could we all possibly go? No matter where we hide there is nowhere in the Compound where we won't be found. We can hide here and there but eventually they'll find us. I don't see anyway out of this."

"Look Essa, there is a way out!" Raeban spoke gently to his mother. "Meeyha and I have seen the way out. There is even a conveyance that can hold more than two people. We could all get to where the conveyance is housed and leave the compound. I had even received a message from White that he was at the Cleansing Quarters and that he thought we were in danger. So, you see, we have to get out of here and we know how. We just have to get out of the building, follow the tunnel to the Cleansing Quarters then take the conveyance out of the compound. We can do it! I know we can!"

They all remained still in the small room. Banner, oblivious to everything around him, was as still as a corpse. The others, all aware of the danger they were in, remained frozen in their tracks: their hearts beating so hard that their bodies quivered with each beat. As they stood in the room, undecided as to their immediate strategy, foot steps could be heard outside the door. As before Raeban tensed and quietly urged everyone to hide. While they waited the foot steps went past, stopped, then turned around and headed back. The door pushed slowly open. A white head peered in and saw a stretcher crammed in the small room with the two beds. He looked to the head of the stretcher and was astonished to see one of the very persons that he was looking for. "Banner," White spoke quietly, "can you hear me?" Hearing the familiar voice, Meeyha and Raeban came out of their hiding place and breathed an audible sigh as they both rushed to White. Meeyha was so pleased to see him that she threw her arms around him and gave him a kiss on the cheek. The reunion however was all carried on in silence. Raeban quietly explained their predicament to White and asked his opinion.

After hearing all that had happened up till then, White decided that the plan to call Master Svene, was a good one, and would give them the time they needed to make their escape.

Chapter 23

As Master Svene was leaving the Calming Quarters a calm, peaceful feeling seemed to wash over his entire body. Then he thought to himself that that was very appropriate when leaving the Calming Quarters, that one should feel calm and peaceful. He stood on the top step of the entrance to the Calming Quarters and took a deep breath. He remembered how different it was breathing the air outside of this compound. The evenings were always filled with scents from the myriad of flowers and shrubs that adorned the grounds all around his home. And the breezes that would convey those scents were beyond comparing to anything inside the compound. Even the scents from the flowers and shrubs growing all around the Calming Quarters couldn't come close to the heady scents he longed so much to return to.

He continued stroking the white flight feather that he had picked up in the Potting Shed. He couldn't remember what had happened in the Potting Shed but the bird that dropped that feather must have gone through some pretty traumatic experiences to lose such an important feather. He looked up at the sky when he heard a rustle of leaves above him. He saw nothing. 'I can't see anything', he thought. There were no stars in this sky within the compound. The makeup of dome's cover was such that it not only inhibited the penetration of computer signals but it also distorted the passing of light waves through it, making the sky look a milky black. Yes, he thought, he was going to be very happy to leave this place once and for all. As he continued looking upwards he perceived a glow coming from the branches of a small tree just ahead of where he stood. He stepped down, still stroking the feather in his hand, and headed for the table and chairs placed under the small tree. When he came to the last step his foot, to his amazement, didn't touch the ground. His entire body seemed to be as weightless as the feather in his hand. The feather then seemed to pull him towards the table under the tree. He was confused, he no longer had control of his arms or his legs. He could only move his head; and he turned it, to and fro, trying desperately to locate the source of this unusual occurrence. Even his voice was gone, so calling out for help was also beyond his ability.

Then he saw the bird. It was the most beautiful bird he had ever seen. The feathers were a translucent white which glowed brighter the longer that Master Svene looked at it. The bird did not look at Master Svene. It was looking beyond him and the Calming Quarters.

Then, ever so slowly and gently, Master Svene was lowered onto a waiting chair. He looked back at the bird above him then back at his hand holding the feather. He could feel a drop of warm liquid fall onto his hand. He threw the feather from him but it began drifting back towards him, coming closer than before. Finally it stopped just above Master Svene's heart: now beating wildly inside his chest. He watched the bird, unable to do anything else. As he watched the bird it opened its' beak and started to speak.

"Surgical Master Raun: Healing Assistant Sarena: Child Marina: Matron Celeste—" Master Svene gasped when he realized that the bird was calling out names. And those were the names that had just—Master Svene couldn't think. What had happened to Surgical Master Raun and Healing Assistant Sarena? And what about that Child Marina: who was she and what did this have to do with him? And he didn't have anything to do with Matron Celeste, she had gone mad. He was the Master of Masters and no one confronted him. Then he grasped the meaning. the Potting Shed; that's what happened in the Potting Shed.

'No', his brain corrected, 'Surgical Master Raun and Healing Assistant Sarena didn't die in the Potting Shed, only their bodies were in the Potting Shed: but he had been responsible for putting them there.' He, the Master of Masters, was responsible for all their deaths.

As the bird had been calling out the names of the deceased a drop of blood fell from the feather hovering above Master Svene. When he saw the drops of blood pooling onto his tunic Master Svene screamed, then passed out. It had been too much for him. From the euphoria of calmness and peacefulness he plummeted to the depths of fear and despair. The knowledge of all those lives taken to satisfy a selfish desire for perfection, conformity and greed, both humiliated and diminished him.

Each name called and each drop of blood was like another spear piercing his heart. The bird continued calling out names and the blood kept dropping from the feather until the bird fell silent and Master Svene slumped back in his chair, head drooping to his chest, now saturated with the blood of countless people.

"Master Svene! Master Svene!" shouted White when he caught sight of him as he stepped out of the Calming Quarters. The scene that White had witnessed under the small tree was too terrible to behold. Blood covered Master Svene from his shoulders to his feet and was pooling all around him on the ground. The bird was now silent but it still looked beyond the building to some distant place. The feathers were once again becoming a pure white, slowly losing their glowing translucency as it stood on the branch looking down at Master Svene. And Master Svene was as silent and still as a stone. White shook himself to action and hurried over to Master Svene and frantically felt for a pulse. It was faint and weak but it was still there.

White shouted for help as loud as he could. He tried to revive Master Svene as he waited for assistance. But no one came. White left Master Svene where he was and hurried back into the Calming Quarters.

When he had left the others, to go in search of Master Svene, he had no idea what was waiting outside for him. He would never have expected what he found. A bird alone would have been a surprise, to see in the dead of night sitting on the branch of the small tree, but the spectre of blood surrounding an unconscious Master Svene was beyond the unthinkable. For the blood that was visible to the eye was not tangible to the touch. The feather that had dripped blood with each name called, was now hovering above Master Svene's heart, but with no blood evident anywhere on its shaft.

His mind was racing as he hurried through the Calming Quarters to locate the equipment and medications necessary with which to examine and administer to Master Svene. When Essa had been informed that Master Svene had not returned to the Cleansing Quarters, it had again sent the group into a anxious state. They were afraid to remain in the small room for fear of being found and they were reluctant to leave it for the same reason. It had been necessary then for some action. White decided that looking for Master Svene was the best way to tackle the situation. He knew, also, that he was the only one with enough authority to approach Master Svene if there were a confrontation in the works.

White had a moment of trepidation when he heard that Master Svene had returned to the Cleansing Quarters, for Bianca herself had returned to the Cleansing Quarters. It had been decided that arrangements should be made with Valtre for the operation of the conveyance and also for the possibility of retrieving the Archives containing the compound's most vital information. If the authorities outside the compound were going to help identify the families in the compound, the

Archives were a crucial tool. The search, any other way, would be overwhelming and the proof of the extent of the atrocities that had been done could not be substantiated. Thus White was ambivalent in his endeavour to revive Master Svene. But his oath to protect and preserve life was too precious for him to violate. He continued on, never once hesitating in his course of action.

Finally he found what he needed and turned to rush back to Master Svene's side. He literally flew out the door with the equipment weighing him down causing him to slip as he headed down the steps. He slid, arms extended, right in the direction of the chair that Master Svene had collapsed in. He cringed as he anticipated sliding into the pool of blood but to his surprise, the ground was dry. He quickly picked himself up, and groaned as he noticed the equipment that he had been carrying, strewn, in pieces at the bottom of the steps.

White's eyes fell to Master Svene and his heart skipped a beat when he noticed that Master Svene's head was raised and he was looking, with focused intent, up to the bird perched in the tree. Only then did White realize that the bird was speaking, for its beak and head were posturing as if in conversation. He also noticed that the feather that had been dripping blood onto Master Svene earlier, was now transferring the blood back up into its shaft. There were now but a few drops of blood still remaining on the breast of Master Svene's tunic.

White was mesmerized. What he heard was unbelievable. If he wasn't witnessing this himself he would never believe either the scene or the conversation transpiring. The bird opened his beak again and reiterated to Master Svene, "You are forgiven, but now you must make things right for all those that have been wronged: starting with you sister." Master Svene replied, "But I wasn't the one that started it all. I didn't even know I had a sister. My father didn't even have a partner in the compound." To which the bird countered, "That is irrelevant! Forgiveness must also come from those you have wronged and those wronged by your father. Once you make things right for them then you can go back to your family." With the last words the bird opened its wings wide and the feather, which had remained hovering during all the proceedings, was returned to its place along the other flight feathers. The bird flapped his wings in place on the branch then gracefully lifted upwards and flew into the darkness over the Calming Quarters and out of sight.

White and Master Svene both continued looking in the direction the bird flew in, not really expecting it to come back but unable to believe that it had actually been there and speaking to them. There were birds that talked, but this bird spoke, and he spoke with the authority of one that was accustomed to being in control. They couldn't understand how or why the bird spoke but the impact of its words still resonated in their heads. Finally both men turned and looked at each other: but words deserted them both. All they could do was continue looking at each other, then gradually: at their surroundings. It was pitch black without the glow from the bird to illuminate the scene, but they both looked around to where the blood had pooled onto Master Svene's tunic and the ground about him. There was no evidence anywhere of the blood, there was no wet mark and no stain. Each of them thought that they must have been hallucinating. But the look in each other's eyes confirmed that they both knew what the other had witnessed.

Master Svene was the first to break the silence, "White, thank you for coming to my aid just now. I'm sorry that I couldn't let you know that I was alright. But the bird had quite the control thing going on there—I'm not really sure that I know what it all means but maybe you could help me clear some things up? What do you think?" He spoke with little conviction. He was sure that White was aware of more than he knew. Otherwise White would not be here, outside, at the Calming Quarters, in the middle of the night. He waited for White to speak. But before White could utter a word there began a low rumbling in the ground under their feet. The rumbling grew with intensity, the ground then started to vibrate. Again the vibrating started out very slowly and gently then became stronger and stronger as the trees and shrubs began swaying back and forth. The building itself behind them seemed to sway in time with the trees and shrubs.

People started running out of the building, not really knowing what they should be doing. This was not an earthquake prone area so there were no instructions provided for them to follow. All they could do was look around in horror; the presence of two Masters did little to comfort them. This type of occurrence was unheard of. Their existence in the compound had been totally free of any kind of physical manifestations: no storms, no rain, no wind, no earthquakes.

Then, as they stood looking around in confusion they witnessed the most terrifying phenomenon yet. The fabric of the dome above them started to shake and shudder with cracks becoming visible across their sky. They heard a strange tinkling sound as the dome started to break apart. Pieces of the dome started to fall towards them; but, as the pieces fell to the ground, they began to disintegrate and then became a fine rain. The terrified people again stared in wonder as they reveled in the fine rain, something that they had never before experienced. They were mesmerized as they watched the ground beneath their feet absorb the moisture as it descended. It also accumulated on trees, shrubs, grass, buildings and on the crowd itself standing silent and still. The entire overhead dome had disappeared.

The people continued to stare at their new surroundings in silent wonder. The night sky was now filled with millions of tiny bright lights as far as their eyes could see. To further astound them, a slight breeze began to blow tousling their damp hair and clothes. Gasps and squeals of surprise and delight, at this new sensation, could be heard everywhere in the compound. They began to laugh and hug each other as if they had been waiting for this moment all their lives and were now celebrating its arrival. Emotions flowed freely, but they could no more suppress them than they could change what had just happened around them.

White looked around for Meeyha and Raeban in the mass of humanity that had emerged from the buildings and complexes in the vicinity, but he couldn't spot them. He took a few steps away from where he stood with Master Svene then stopped and went back to where he remained sitting. White took Master Svene's arm and gently prompted him to rise then lead the Master of Masters back inside the Calming Quarters.

Chapter 24

When White had left Meeyha, Raeban, Tabina and Banner, with Essa in the small room, they had feared that the evening would probably end tragically for them all. They waited for a short while, more for courage to accept the inevitable than for any other reason, before beginning any plans to leave the room. What they had all been feeling, in the last few days, had seemed so natural that the emotions and feelings of the moment propelled them to perform as they had. Yet they also felt that they had been compelled by a force outside themselves but which was so ingrained in their beings that all they could do was comply. There were no discordant feelings: it all felt so natural, as if they had lived thus as long as they could remember. So they proceeded. Even the fear itself felt natural. Yet they couldn't explain why.

Now that White had left, to try to bring some semblance of resolution to the manic situation, they decided that they too should go with White to locate the Master of Masters. They couldn't just sit around and wait for their destiny to unfold around them without their own input. So, within minutes they had decided to act. Meeyha and Raeban left first accompanied by Tabina, and Essa followed with the still unconscious Banner. They proceeded with caution but without the immobilizing fear that they had previously experienced. Their minds had been made up, and they would continue to handle each new crisis as it appeared.

Meeyha, Raeban and Tabina took the stairs while Essa and Banner used the elevator to get to the ground floor. Surprisingly, they all reached the ground floor at the same time but as they did so they felt a shutter and shaking of the floor and walls around them. They stood rooted to the spot. What they had experienced resembled the description of an earthquake. Their years at the mega-school had given them that much knowledge. But they all knew that earthquakes had never been considered a problem in this area before.

Raeban called out to them, "wait here for a minute and I'll go check outside and see what's happening." The ground floor landing, on which they had all arrived at the same time, was just at the back door of the Calming Quarters, so Raeban ran the few steps to the door and opened it wide. He looked out at an unchanged landscape except for the swaying, to and fro, of the trees and shrubs that were vaguely apparent in the black night. Their was no one around so Raeban sprinted to the side of the building. To his amazement, there on the street, were more people congregating than he had ever seen in one place before. He motioned to the others, peering from inside the building to follow, then he ran back to help with Banner. They all stopped in their tracks as they saw a beautiful white, glowing bird fill the black night with its brilliance. They stood rooted to the spot as they watched the bird settle on one of the upwards outstretched arms of the child, in the memorial, at the back of the grounds. The bird then spread its wings as it stood on the child's arm. A glow began to gradually appear from the centre of the monument, at about the point of the child's feet. The glow moved upwards and slowly floated into the blackness of the night sky. They continued watching, mesmerized, as more glowing figures followed the first.

The figures had the look of human forms but they were made up entirely of glowing light. Their appendages were very long and lanky and trailed slightly beyond the normal length of a human form. Their faces were tilted upwards to a destination beyond and remained so until they reached the top of the dome. The group watching, heard the sound of breaking glass as the figures drifted to the domes' edge with the fabric of the dome cracking and crumbling with their approach. The group couldn't believe what they were seeing but they no longer felt any fear. The presence of the bird and figures had instilled a calm and peacefulness within them as they watched the scene unfolding. As the figures continued their upwards journey the assembly observed the disintegration of their sky but all they felt with this new phenomenon was liberation and a sense of release. They had, none of them, ever experienced such emotions before. A gentle rain began to fall onto them and brought them back to the moment. Meeyha and Raeban started to laugh and opened their arms in welcome of this new event and looked around to see Tabina and Essa doing the same.

To their surprise, Banner, looking upwards as he sat in his wheelchair, arms outstretched, called out to the floating figures, "fly: fly: you're free at last!" They didn't know if it was to the bird or to the figures that he directed the words, but when they realized that he had come to and was totally coherent they all converged on him at once. Banner got up from his chair and took Tabina in his arms and hugged her close for a very long time. The others watched, tears now flowing freely, as the enormity of the situation finally took effect. They began hugging each other, their tears mingling as their lives had mingled so intimately, in the last few hours. At this point the bird flapped its wings and lifted majestically into the air.

When they finally released each other and looked around they noticed that the last of the figures were just disappearing into the sky and that millions of tiny lights suddenly appeared in their place. They could hear the squeals and laughter of the others, at the front of the Calming Quarters, as the rain and the breeze stirred their senses.

Then, as if on cue, Meeyha and Raeban began running around to the side of the building, with the others close behind, to see the mass of humanity laughing and dancing in celebration. None was concerned about the rain, or about what they must look like: they simply enjoyed the feelings that had been suppressed for so long.

Raeban remembered that White wasn't with them and pulled Meeyha close to ask her assistance in locating him. They also requested Essa, Tabina and Banner for their help in the search, but Essa immediately spotted White escorting Master Svene back into the Calming Quarters. She indicated the direction in which White was headed so they started towards the building and followed White and Svene inside. Apprehension took hold as they entered the building but proceeded none the less. There was nothing for them to fear any longer. Looking around them they saw that things had changed for good. Everything that they had lived and known for so long had altered. They couldn't know what was to happen but what they did know was that great change was coming and that this time, of elation and abandon, would help them to deal with what was to come.

As they proceeded into the Calming Quarters they observed White and Master Svene sitting in the reception area, still and silent. It was like they were waiting for the group to arrive for they both became animated when the group entered.

"Good, you're all here," began White "There is much that we must discuss, so please, make yourselves comfortable, it's going to be a long night."

Waiting patiently beside White, Master Svene then interjected "First of all, before we get started, I would like to offer my deepest apologies to you all but especially to you, Tabina," he uttered as he turned to face her. He extended his hands and waited for her response. For a few seconds Tabina just stared at Svene, no expression or word gave away her feelings.

"I know that you must have a million questions, and I would like to say that I will try to answer them as best I can," began Svene a second time as he continued to hold his hands extended. Still she stood still and silent, her tall form almost the height of Master Svene himself. As she continued looking at him her face finally registered what appeared to be surprise and recognition then tentatively extended her own hand. Master Svene gently took her hand and covered it with his own. "Tabina, I am your brother and I have caused you, and your partner here, much pain and suffering. Can you forgive what I have done to you and your partner?"

Tabina thought for another few moments then responded, "I can only guess at what I am expected to forgive because no one has explained why we were brought here." Her voice held no accusations but she spoke with a calm, strong voice. "Banner and I were spirited away, when we asked for the right to care for our own child, and never once did we receive a response to any of our questions. Would you answer now, why we, any of us, are not allowed to raise our own children?"

Svene was taken aback. He expected some hesitation to his request but he had been unprepared for her directness. His recovery was immediate as he explained that it had been thus for centuries, and that it was best, for all involved, that children should be raised without the intense, sometimes smothering, nurturing by the natural parents. The children were raised to develop to their utmost potential and thus contributing to the ongoing success of the community of which they were a member.

"Natural parents are not always the best authority to determine what potential the child holds." Master Svene explained calmly, now to the group in general.

But Tabina could not just accept the explanation. "That may be true, but for thousands of years before our community as you call it, parents had been raising their own children. Why did this community feel that they knew better than the billions that had come before them?" Master Svene could see that receiving forgiveness was going to be harder than he had anticipated so he changed his approach.

"Tabina, what has happened is all in the past, but I would like to try to set things right now, for you and for everyone else here. What I am offering you, though, is the opportunity to be a part of my family so that we can return to what we should never have tampered with. Will you help me to make this possible for the rest of those here?"

As expected, Tabina could not refuse what, in effect, she had been hoping for since the birth of her first child. She smiled and shook the hands that were still holding hers. "Hello, brother. Now, of course, you must know who my parents were so I will expect you to divulge all."

"You have my word Tabina, that you will get all the information that we have. Not just for you, but for everyone one here, in this room, and in the whole compound. Our records have been impeccable, thus we can find out everyone's ancestors right back to the beginning of this community. It won't be easy or fast, but it can be done and it will." Svene suddenly felt a huge weight lift from his being. He felt as light as a feather and the love that he felt for his family outside the compound now extended to this new member.

Meeyha and Raeban looked at each other as they held hands then both closed around Essa as she stood silently crying beside them. Mother and son held each other and cried tears of joy and the love of a family reunited.

Tabina and Banner both took turns hugging Svene, Tabina's newly found half-brother. White looked on in wonder as he realized what had just happened. He could now see the family resemblances of the people around them. Of course Tabina and Svene were blood related. The blond hair, the blue eyes, the tall towering forms, that were a rarity in the community, were all evidence that they were indeed related. Then he looked at Meeyha and Raeban. Raeban looked just like his mother, only with masculine features. The raven black hair, the big deep golden eyes with the dark edges and the shape of the face, the evidence was there for all to see. His smile faded for a brief moment as he thought about Coral and his lost child, but then he remembered Bianca who had been his original selected partner and his heart filled with new hope and new love. This was going to be wonderful. He had felt in his heart that everything would change eventually, he just hadn't realized that he would be alive to see it for himself or that he himself would be involved in the change. White smiled again, he had seen the worst happen, but now he could see the best coming. Love, compassion, peace and forgiveness was here for them all.

The work ahead of them was going to be colossal but with Bianca's archives, and the recorded births, deaths, of everyone in the compound, since its inception, would not only be possible, but it would also be accurate and complete.

Eight Months Later

Meeyha and Raeban named their twin babies Marina, for the little girl that had become one of Master Svene's casualties, and Tanner, the name of Raeban's father, whom he had never met nor would he ever know. They were born almost five months to the day that the world, as they knew it, came to an end.

They couldn't believe how their lives had changed after the birth of those two perfect little squirming babies. Happiness never held such a meaning as it did with the children's birth and the knowledge now that there were also other people that they were tied to by virtue of genetics. Their lives now seemed complete and fulfilled with these new experiences.

The archives had located family for Meeyha. Some were long gone but she had found a sister, right here in the compound, with whom she had spoken to and liked during her episode in the Calming Quarters. It was none other than Viki. They took to each other as if they had been interacting all their lives. Viki, just a year younger than Meeyha, proved to be not only a loving aunt for Meeyha's two children but indispensable in her knowledge and care of the children. They were together constantly.

Raeban and his mother were bonding too. Slower than Essa would have liked but she was happy none the less for having the opportunity of reuniting with her son. But she was even more grateful for her role as grandmother to her two beautiful grandchildren. They were the love of her life.

Another surprise was that Valtre, Viki's partner, was White's nephew. White was ecstatic, he had almost given up ever finding any blood relatives, but there he was, now so close to White's young friends that they all seemed like one big happy family.

Bianca's family had all been eradicated. It apparently had been a deliberate action when Bianca's forceful, intense and unbending characteristics had been noticed as a child. The Masters felt that it would be best that they keep the younger, more valuable member close, in order to make the most of her brilliant mind. And with her passion for organization, and the safety and concern for the archives, it became even more imperative that she have no distractions from her cause. The Masters had been pleased with their decisions.

Tabina had reconciled with her half-brother and had been introduced to Svene's family outside the dome. She had taken to her half-brother's family just as if they had been her own, but was euphoric when her own two children were found and returned to her. She had forgiven Svene that night in the Calming Quarters for reducing her to a barren desert, but all that had been completely forgotten when she met her two young, beautiful, children. They both carried her genes: bright yellow hair and tall graceful bodies with the demeanour of royalty.

Banner had only three cousins within the compound, but it turned out that one of the founding fathers had been a great, great, great, great grandfather, who had been instrumental in making sure that the children were only cared for by the most compassionate and loving people. He had been known as 'Karl the Kind' by his peers.

Most of the people had decided to remain in the compound. It was all they had known so it would take them many years to adjust to the notion of an outside world. The younger individuals had been offered instructions in whatever field they required to prepare them for the future, within or outside the dome, and the older populace was given the opportunity of continuing to live within the compound as before.

Meeyha, Raeban, and all his newly found family, had decided to remain and prepare themselves before leaving the dome and venturing out into an unfamiliar world. But when they did leave, they would all leave as a unit. Family and friends had become the most important things in their lives and they were never going to jeopardize those unions for anything.

The End

GLOSSARY

<u>Calming Master</u>: equivalent to psychologists.

<u>Calming Quarters</u>: a building where operations were performed and where one was sent if not coping psychologically.

<u>Compound</u>: the area encompassed by the 'dome' under which all the complexes, healing centres and the mega-schools are located.

<u>Conveyance</u>: a vehicle, powered by an internal power generating cell, for the purpose of traveling long distances within the dome, usually restricted to the upper level masters and which travel at slow speeds.

<u>Dome</u>: a highly technical collection of clear orbs connected over the entire compound which simulates a sky and creating a terrarium type environment with a very mild climate and no overhead precipitation.

<u>Eden Project</u>: the original name of the compound as given by the founding fathers implying that this was a totally new world.

E.R.U.: Emergency Rescue Unit, equivalent to an Ambulance.

Elite Masters: usually Masters holding a Level 1, 2, or 3 status (a higher number indicated higher education, responsibility and power).

Food stores: building from which crops and food stuffs are processed, stored, and distributed throughout the compound.

Governing Masters: the Masters in charge of making the laws and the conduct that was expected by the inhabitants of the compound.

Healing assistant: similar to nurses.

Healing Centre: a building where one was sent for minor physical problems and recuperation after surgery

Healing Master: physician, or general practitioner.

Healing Masters Level 1, Level 2, or Level 3: Physicians/ surgeons/ psychiatrist (or other members of the governing body) possessing superior credentials

Initiating the Young: a place where children, under the age of 2, are sent to be taught personal hygiene and social interaction until they are ready for to the mega-school.

Jobbers: individuals that did odd jobs which did not require advanced skills but are still necessary to perform.

Keeper of the Archives: the most important position within the compound after the Master of Masters. This is the person responsible for entering and protecting the births, deaths, and pairings within the compound.

Leave to travel: request to travel outside of the individual's resident complex.

Library: establishment where a collection of early civilization books are housed and protected with great care, (accessible only to the Masters).

Masters in Charge: a group of people that would be equivalent to police.

Masters: the group of people intense and driven to re-create a new human experience, with no wars, pollution or environmental impacts.

Masters of Neurosurgery: the Masters that performed the surgery necessary, to create docile compliant beings, shortly after birth.

Mega-school: an education facility that also houses all the children between the ages of 2 and 14 years, until they enter into a career or job.

Norm: Standards, as set down by the Masters in charge of the mega-school.

Nutrition Bank: the building where all the food products are kept until required for distribution.

Nutrition Room: a room in each unit used for preparing and consuming food.

Nurturing Quarters: where newborns are sent for rearing and educating until the age of 2 when they are sent to the mega-school.

Parents: people provided to care for the newborns in nurturing, structured facilities in order to encourage optimum potential from the pupils.

Personal Communicator: a multi-purpose device that enables communication with others as well as serving as G.P.S. message centre, information source (much like current cell phones with aps).

Post-peace era: the time before the Masters took over a portion of the human race and forced the peace and environmental protection agendas.

Primary Instructors: under-Masters who instruct the 2 years olds at the mega-school.

Retro-dreaming: the dreaming about what happened in the past without having any knowledge of the past history.

Revered Aged Ones: one of the Masters who had served their term as required, in an advanced field, and is then able to enjoy retirement with no concerns of any kind.

The Potting Shed: a small building, adjoining the main Calming Quarters building, which was used to house the gardener's paraphernalia among other more sinister chores such as reducing the corpses to ashes which were then used as fertilizer for the shrubs and flowers around the premises.

They: the pronoun used to collectively refer to the Masters.

Under-Master: an individual that was being groomed for progression towards being a Master in any given field within the compound.

Work: the position held by each individual providing a service or benefit necessary within the complex or compound thus providing all the necessities of life to that individual.

CPSIA information can be obtained at www.ICGtesting.com
Printed in the USA
LVOW062036081211
258496LV00001B/39/P